GRAVES FOR THE LIVING

Eric stumbled over the gravestone, crashed to the ground, and saw the crossbow skitter out of his hands and disappear over the edge of the open grave. In the moonless night the grave was black, like a gaping mouth. Eric felt an involuntary chill climb his spine as he reached into the hole, groping blindly for his weapon.

He touched only black fetid air.

Flattening his body against the ground he plunged his arm further in the hole. His hand touched cold metal—and with relief he wrapped his fingers around the crossbow's stock. The crossbow was still cocked, ready for action.

Suddenly, from within the grave, a hand closed around Eric's wrist. Another hand grabbed his forearm, long ragged nails digging into his skin. A third hand clutched his crossbow. Then all three hands yanked at once and Eric tumbled backward into the dark grave. . . .

THE
WARLORD #5
TERMINAL ISLAND
BY JASON FROST

ZEBRA BOOKS
KENSINGTON PUBLISHING CORP.

To Michael and Barbara Frost, friends before there ever was a Warlord.

ZEBRA BOOKS

are published by

Kensington Publishing Corp.
475 Park Avenue South
New York, NY 10016

First printing: November 1985

Printed in the United States of America

Book One:

THE GRAVEROBBERS

*Where lies the final harbor, whence we unmoor
no more?*

Herman Melville

1

The cemetery was dark. Moonless. They groped blindly among the broken and overturned tombstones. Around the open graves.

"Whose idea was this?" D.B. asked, her voice pinched with fear.

"We're almost through it," Eric Ravensmith assured her. "It's the safest way through this part of the city."

"What city? There's nothing left but some hobo shacks, a Howard Johnson's motel, and two collapsed gas stations. Everything else is ashes."

"Except for this cemetery."

"Didn't I thank you for the tour?"

He watched her carefully. Even at only eighteen she didn't frighten easily. But she was frightened now. Graveyards did that to people.

Eric's foot bumped something hard. A lifesize statue of an angel half-buried in the dirt. Her head and one wing were broken off. Someone had spray-painted a red target where her crotch was and red splotches for nipples. Eric stepped over her. "There were campfires at those other places. That means people. We're trying to avoid people, remember? The kind of people who would do this." He nudged the broken angel with his foot.

"I know, I know. You're right. I'm not superstitious or anything but this place is spooky. When I was a kid, even Casper the Friendly Ghost used to scare me. That big bald head of his reminded me of Telly Savalas." She jumped over another open grave. "You have any idea where we are?"

"Sure," Eric said. "Lost."

She stopped, grabbed his arm. "You're joking, right?"

"Yes, I'm joking. Calm down, will you? We're fine." Eric heard her fidget with the thick metal choke collar around her neck. The one they'd made her wear as a slave back when he'd first seen her, when they'd paraded her around on a dog leash. He'd tried to talk her into throwing it away, but she insisted on keeping it as a reminder of what she'd been through before Eric had rescued her. That the horror could easily happen again. Her "reality rosary" she called it.

"You know what this place reminds me of?" D.B. asked.

"What?"

"That video of Michael Jackson's 'Thriller.' The one with the dancing ghouls and stuff. You ever see that?"

"Once or twice," Eric said. He kept moving, trying to fight the memory. No use. Like all the memories of his past it came to him with almost physical pain, as if it were clawing out through his chest. Chewing through his heart and ribs and flesh. And like the others memories, it was so damn vivid. He could feel the warmth of their breath, see the glistening of their eyes, smell the sweet shampoo in their hair. He saw them all in the living room watching MTV. His wife Annie dragging the kids, Jenny and Tim, to their feet and dancing with them, clumsily imitating Michael

Jackson's smooth twirling steps. The three of them hopping around Eric's chair, making vampire faces and collapsing in a laughing heap on top of him. Annie nipping at his neck, whispering huskily, "Bet you can't eat just one." Jenny pointing at the TV, saying, "I hate it when a boy's prettier than me." Timmy responding with, "Then you must hate all the boys." Jenny, sticking her finger out at him like a gun and burping. They had all laughed.

That was then.

This was now.

And now Annie and Jenny were dead. Murdered. Tim kidnapped.

All by the same man. Colonel Dirk Fallows, Eric's ex-commanding officer from Vietnam. The one Eric had testified against and put in jail. The one they were now trailing. Just Eric and a skinny teenager hunting the Albert Einstein of killers. Eric shook his head at the absurdity.

He stepped over an open grave, his foot crunching down on something hard, brittle. He bent closer for a look. It was a severed hand, chopped off at the wrist. Most of the gray flesh had decomposed or been eaten away. The thin bones of the fingers showed through white as teeth.

"Where's the rest of him?" D.B. asked, examining the hand.

"Probably dragged off by animals."

"Or people?"

Eric shrugged. They'd seen some cannibalism up around Santa Barbara, some out in the desert. But it was still rare. So far. "Looks like a clean cut at the wrist. Could be from the shovel that dug her up."

"Graverobbers?"

"Maybe." Eric rested against a nearby gravestone. He wasn't tired but he could tell D.B. was shaken and

9

needed a minute to compose herself. The hard stone felt cool against his shoulder. Thick as grief. Even in the dark he could read some of the chiseled words. *Beloved. Maria Theresa. Loving child.* Whoever Maria Theresa was, the graverobbers had gotten her too. Nothing was left of the loving child but a deep empty hole.

D.B. sat on the overturned gravestone, tucked her knees under her chin. "This place looks like some gopher city. They must've dug up every damn grave here."

"Just about."

"Shit man." She lobbed a pebble into the dark. It clicked against an unseen gravestone. "Think that's what happened to my dad? Think some scavengers came along and rooted through the ground just so they could strip him of his clothing or jewelry or any goddamn thing they could find?"

"I don't know."

An angry sob caught in her throat. "Think that's what happened to your family?"

"No," Eric said.

"How can you be so damn sure?"

Eric looked her in the eyes. "I burned the bodies."

D.B. paused, thinking that over. "That was smart, Doc Rock. Yeah. That way there's nothing for you to go back to. Nothing they can take away. That's what it's all about these days, isn't it?"

Eric stood up. She was right, of course, but it saddened him that she understood such a grim lesson so well at her age. But that's what California had become since the quakes had cut it off from the rest of the world and sealed it under the deadly poisonous dome of the Long Beach Halo. It had become one giant grave. And the survivors were all robbers, looting the dead and dying, burying the ideals that no longer worked in this world.

Eric walked off into the dark. He'd done his share of looting. Burying too. "Let's go."

"I second that emotion," D.B. said, hopping to her feet. She was shifting into her peppy mode, trying to fight her fear through chatter. "It's weird, man. We've seen a lot worse stuff than this, but something about all these open graves gives me the creeps. Even the words. Grave. Tomb. Jesus, tooooomb. Sounds like a dark tunnel with a giant hairy spider in it."

"Yeah," Eric said, "or the place under your bed when you were a kid."

She nodded. "That knocks me out the way you think of things at your age."

Eric stepped carefully around an open grave. At 35, he didn't consider himself ancient. But he knew what she meant and merely smiled. Talking seemed to calm her down, so he kept the patter up while he hurried her through the cemetery. "A tomb used to be nothing more than the house the deceased had lived in."

"You mean when you died they just stuck you in your own house to rot?"

"Yup. Sealed you up and left you. They even stocked it with clothes and utensils so the dead would have everything they needed in the next world."

"Like a Walkman and some Hall and Oates tapes."

"Something like that."

She thought that over. "What would you take? I mean, what would you want buried with you for the next world?"

That's easy, he thought. Annie. That's all he wanted in this world or the next. "That's easy," he said. "A copy of *Moby Dick*. The Beatles' *White Album*. A carton of Thomas's English muffins. Love those nooks and crannies."

D.B. laughed. "You're weird."

"Me? Some of the royal dead had their servants put to death and buried with them to serve in the next life. Queen Shub-Ad of Ur in Mesopotamia had sixty servants killed so they could serve her for eternity."

"Talk about job security."

"Most of what we know about ancient civilizations comes from what we found in those tombs."

D.B. stopped walking, surveyed the acres of rutted graves. She sighed sadly. "This place is sure gonna tell future people a lot about us, huh?"

Eric didn't answer. He had seen worse in Vietnam. The bodies of dead GIs stripped naked and plowed into the fields for fertilizer. Their blood soaking into the soil. Later whenever he had eaten mango or jackfruit, he had wondered if it had been nourished by the blood of his dead buddies. After a while, he'd stopped wondering and just ate.

That was a lesson he hadn't taught his students at the University back when he was Dr. Ravensmith, associate professor of history. Back when he bicycled across a green campus, not hiked through open graves.

That was a different world.

It was hard to believe that on the other side of the Long Beach Halo, people still lived as he once had. Watched television, went to movies, ate at restaurants, flirted, worried about their skin, their hemlines, their ties being straight, shoes polished. Their weight.

Eric looked up. The thick smoky Halo that prevented them from leaving and others from entering, enclosed the island of California like a helmet. Passing through the Halo meant disfigurement or death. On the other side, U.S. gunships waited to turn back any who tried to escape the island. The outside world feared contamination, a modern-day plague. Eric didn't blame them.

Still, from inside the Halo it looked eerily beautiful. The moon was a long splotch of white, like a wound, a rip in the gray flannel sky.

"There!" D.B. said excitedly. "Look!" She had her glasses on and was pointing across the cemetery.

Eric saw it immediately. The hole. The shovel handles stuck in the mound of dirt. An unlit lantern. He could smell the sweet cloying scent of freshly dug earth. He unslung his crossbow from his back, cocked it, and inserted a sharp bolt.

D.B. pulled out a huge 9mm Astra A-80, 36 ounces of steel with a 15-round magazine. She released the safety.

They crouched behind a gravestone.

"Graverobbers?" D.B. whispered.

"Looks like it. But where are they?"

"Maybe they left for the night. Even graverobbers gotta sleep. Though I don't know how they can."

Eric looked around for some sign of movement, listened for a sound. Nothing. Damn, why hadn't he been more careful? The cemetery had seemed so picked over he didn't think anyone would still be hanging around here. What was left to steal?

"Let's take a look," D.B. said, starting to rise.

"No." Eric held her back.

"Why not?"

"It's none of our business. We'll skirt around the edges."

She spun around, her eyes fierce, the dirt on her face streaked with tears. "That's easy for you to say. You barbecued your family. We aren't all so damn clever. I still have a mother somewhere. Maybe alive, maybe not. Maybe in that grave." She bolted from

13

him, running across the field, leaping open graves, zagging around fallen gravestones.

Eric ran after her.

He jumped over a smashed gravestone, but when his foot landed, it hit a chunk of broken granite. His foot turned under as the rest of his 175 pounds came crashing down on it. He felt the muscles stretch and the bones crackle as he tumbled to the ground. His crossbow slid out of his hand and over the edge of an open grave.

"Damn," he muttered. He climbed to his feet, bounced a little on his ankle. Pain sizzled up the leg like a lit fuse. It wasn't broken, probably not even sprained. Just twisted, which hurt even more. He limped over to the dark grave and looked in.

All black. Like a gaping mouth.

Eric felt an involuntary chill climb his spine as he knelt next to the grave. Slowly he reached into the hole, his hand patting blindly for his crossbow.

He touched only black air.

He reached deeper, flattening his body against the ground. More air. Hot fetid air, like the inside of an aluminum garbage can. He plunged his arm and shoulder further into the dark hole.

His hand bumped something solid.

He felt around, sensing its shape.

A body.

It was a chest, a man's chest. The shirt was stiff with dried dirt, torn in places. Apparently they hadn't yet stripped this corpse. The flesh was surprisingly warm, though the hot grave could act as an oven during the day. Eric's hand tramped across the body, knocked into the cold metal of his crossbow. It was still cocked, the safety on. He felt relief as he wrapped his fingers around the stock.

Behind him, D.B.'s scream shredded the silence.

He turned his head, saw her standing in front of the distant open grave. Her gun dropped from her hands as she stumbled backward in terror.

Eric started to his feet, hauling the crossbow up with him.

Suddenly, from within the grave, a hand closed around Eric's wrist. Another hand grabbed his forearm, long ragged nails digging into his skin.

A third hand clutched his crossbow.

All three hands yanked at once and Eric tumbled backward into the dark grave.

As he fell, he heard D.B. still screaming.

2

Eric fell backward into the grave.

As he dropped through the darkness, a fourth hand clamped onto his hair and jerked his head back. The long-nailed hand around his forearm let go and immediately punched him in the neck. Eric felt as if he were being chewed and swallowed by a starving reptile.

It was a short fall, barely five feet. But the groping hands, the sour smell, the black marble darkness recalled old childhood images of zombies. The Late Late Show with the living dead walking stiffly out of the swamps, slimy arms straight and reaching, hungry to enbrace those still alive.

Impact was sudden. Eric's backpack cushioned him as he collided on top of one of the bodies fighting him. A loud "Ummph!" sounded in Eric's ear. The body beneath him writhed, pushing at him. Suddenly sharp teeth sank into Eric's shoulder, scraped against bone.

"Ow!" Eric winced, then snapped his elbow backward. A jaw bone cracked and the teeth released his shoulder.

"Bastard!" someone next to him cried.

Eric felt a large fist strike him in the cheek. It glanced off the cheekbone, but he could feel a tender knob rising under the skin. He pulled at his crossbow, trying to wrestle it from whoever was clutching it. No good.

There were two of them, that much he knew. And they felt pain like living men, not zombies.

The grave was dug like an overturned telephone booth. Long and narrow. Eric couldn't turn without bumping them, without them grabbing at him. He felt a handful of fingers claw at his face, the stubby thumbs trying to gouge out his eyes. Eric swung his left knee around, felt the kneecap sink into the soft flesh of a stomach, graze a protruding rib cage. The fingers at his eyes fell away.

Eric twisted round and felt the hot rancid breath of the other man puffing on him. Instantly he rammed his head forward. The man's nose flattened against his face and blood snorted out of each nostril. The man's sticky blood splashed onto Eric's forehead. Eric rammed him again. The man moaned and his grip loosened on the crossbow.

In one swift movement, Eric straddled the man's chest, shoved the crossbow against his throat, released the safety, and pulled the trigger. The bolt speared through the man's jugular and burrowed into the ground, nailing the attacker to the bottom of the grave.

Eric turned. His eyes had adjusted enough that he could barely make out the outline of the other man struggling to his feet, hugging the wall of the grave for support. But before Eric could get up, the man launched himself, knocking Eric off the dead attacker and into the other wall of the grave.

Two hard blows to the back of Eric's head sent him face-first into the dirt wall. He tasted the dry soil mixed with his own blood like a gritty paste. A heavy fist sank into his kidney. He tried to hold himself up by digging his fingers into the dirt wall of the grave.

"Fucking piece of shit," the man said and threw another punch into Eric's spine. Eric dropped to his knees.

One hand was still sunk knuckle-deep in the dirt wall. He tried to pull himself up. Some of the dirt flaked loose and pelted his hair and face. As he slowly rose, Eric reached back and pulled a bolt from the quiver strapped to his belt. The arrow was hand-made, carved from the branch of a pine tree, tipped with a point hammered from copper tubing he'd ripped from an abandoned refrigerator, and fixed with vinyl feathers cut from the dashboard of a rusted Datsun. He turned just as another punch slammed into his sternum, throwing him hard against the dirt wall. He thrust the bolt straight out into the darkness and leaned into it with all his weight.

At first he thought he'd missed altogether. The arrow passed through several feet of darkness without touching anything. Then there was a slight resistance. Just a little, like biting into Jell-o.

"Ahhh!" the man yowled as the arrow poked into his abdomen, just a few inches above the crotch. The man was standing at an angle, his fist cocked, so the arrow scraped along the pelvic bone before lodging in the spine in the lumbar region, wedged between two vertebrae. A long raspy exhale of sour breath washed over Eric as the man fell to his knees, reached for Eric, then collapsed. Dead.

Eric knelt next to the corpse, yanked the bolt free, and reloaded his crossbow. Next he twisted the bolt from the other man's throat. Each arrow had taken him half an hour to make and he wasn't about to leave them behind.

For an instant it flickered through his mind that he had just killed two men whose faces he never saw clearly, even in death. If he was shown a high school class photo of either, he wouldn't be able to pick them out.

He stood slowly, peering over the edge of the grave. The lantern was now lit so he could see each of them clearly.

Three men were dragging D.B. by her legs toward the large open grave she'd spotted earlier. She slid along on her back, her sweat shirt bunched up around her breasts, her arms flailing uselessly, clutching at the dirt. Her glasses were askew.

D.B. kicked out at one of them, the heel of her New Balance running shoes tearing a three-inch gash in his cheek.

"Got you that time, Carl," one of the others laughed.

"Admit it, Carl," the other one said. "Girls just don't like your face."

"I know I don't," the first one chuckled.

Carl dabbed at the blood on his cheek. "Dumb cunt!" he spat and kicked D.B. hard in the stomach. The impact flipped her over, face-down. The two men, each pulling one leg, exchanged legs and continued dragging her backward, face-down in the dirt. D.B. vomited, leaving a trail of half-digested squirrel stew leading to the grave.

"You dumb fuck, Carl. You better not have damaged her." The man pulling her left leg shook his head. He was bare-chested but wore leather driving gloves. His hair was short and spiked, as if it had been cut by a dull knife. "If you've cracked a rib, we won't get as much."

"How much is she worth, Tommy?" the other man asked. He wore a white tuxedo jacket over his t-shirt and jeans. He had wavy blonde hair that he was obviously very pleased with.

Tommy shrugged. "She's young, that's good. But she's bony, that's bad. Deena will know better. She'll bring at least six cans of beans and a couple of cartons of cigarettes. We'll be able to tell more once we strip off her clothes and give her a workout."

"Me first," Carl barked, rubbing his bloody cheek.

"You first," Eric said to himself as he crawled out of the grave. He dashed for cover behind a nearby gravestone, his ankle still sore with every step. He dropped to one knee and shouldered the crossbow. "Here, Carl. Catch." He fired.

The bolt punched into Charl's chest, knocking him off his feet. "Goddamn!" Carl shouted. He sat up, stared at the bolt, and started tugging on it as if it were nothing more than an annoying splinter. With a powerful jerk, he pulled it out of his chest, stood up, took two shaky steps, and died in mid-stride. He flopped to the ground.

Tommy released D.B.'s left leg and reached for one of the shovel handles stuck in the dirt mound next to the huge grave. But when he plucked the handle from the dirt, it wasn't a shovel but a spear. A long serrated knife had been lashed to the handle with rawhide shoelaces. "Over there!" he shouted, throwing his spear in Eric's direction.

Eric ducked back behind the gravestone just as the spear thunked into the polished marble. He cocked his crossbow again and slipped in another bolt.

The man in the white tuxedo dropped D.B.'s other leg and pulled her 9mm Astra A-80 from his drooping jeans and blasted away at Eric. Chips of stone flicked down on Eric's back.

Eric dove to the other side of the gravestone, somersaulted once and came up with the crossbow jammed against his hip for steadiness. He fired the bolt, which stabbed into the gunman's side, twirling him around and dumping him on the ground. Even so, he kept wildly firing the gun, at Eric, at the air, at anything. "Get him!" he shouted between rounds. "Kill the son of a bitch!"

Eric ducked behind the gravestone again and cocked his crossbow.

Only this time when he reached back for a fresh bolt, he felt a sudden sharp pressure in his back, something hard and painful digging into his shoulder blade. The pain rocked him off-balance and the hard sharp thing pulled free.

Eric looked up, saw the spear tip dripping with his own blood. Saw the young boy, maybe sixteen, standing there grinning, his face smeared with dirt and mud. The spear was a mop handle with a brass letter opener strapped to it.

Behind the boy he saw others coming, each jumping up out of an open grave. Some ran, some walked slowly.

All were armed with crude weapons.

All were coming at Eric.

3

The one-eyed woman frowned. "Is he dead?"

The young boy poked his homemade spear at the unconscious body. "He looks dead."

"Is he *dead?*" she repeated impatiently.

The boy dropped to his knees and suctioned his ear against the broad chest. He listened carefully. "There's something thumping around in there."

The one-eyed woman knelt next to the prone body. She pressed her fingertips under his jaw bone, feeling for a pulse. The kerosene lantern next to the open grave lit her face with an orange glow. Aside from the missing eye, she was also missing an ear. The other had been removed neatly and close to the face. That and having the missing eye on the same side of her head made one side of her face look streamlined, slightly reptilian. She wore her blonde hair pulled back into a tight pony tail as if daring someone to comment on her face. She wore no eyepatch over the scarred socket of the missing eye. The thick ridges of white scar tissue crisscrossed the empty crater like the footprint of a hawk.

She tried the pulse. "Not dead," she said. She reached out and touched his face, her long slender fingers stroking over his closed eyes. Slowly they trailed down his cheeks, his jaw, down to his neck.

There she curled her hands around his throat. She squeezed. Her hands wrung tightly, the thumbs denting the jugular. His eyes snapped open for a desperate moment and he struggled weakly, pawing at her hands. But she kept her grip tight, her teeth grinding as she throttled him. Finally his eyes closed and his mouth went slack.

The one-eyed woman stood up and wiped her hands on her jeans. "Well, he's dead now," she said brightly.

There was only silence from the twenty or so people gathered around.

The kid with the spear nudged her. "Can I have the tux?"

She nodded. "Why not?"

The kid yelped excitedly and dove into the body. He pressed one knee against the chest for leverage and yanked Eric's bolt out. It popped free with a slurping sound. Then he tugged the dirty white tuxedo, only slightly damaged by the arrow hole and blood stain, from the corpse.

The one-eyed woman walked over to Eric and D.B., who stood quietly in front of a dozen ragged guards armed with clubs, spears, hoes, and shovels.

"My husband," the one-eyed woman said, nodding at the dead man. She shrugged. "He lasted longer than the last two. The first died of something we never did figure out. Food poisoning, I guess. Bad can of Hormel chili. The second, Jake, well, he got in a fight with Larry here over that tux. Larry killed Jake. The tux we got from some stiff we dug up over there. Big headstone so he must've been somebody important. Now that I think about it though, it really fit Jake better than Larry."

"Fits me," the young boy said, jumping to his feet and pulling on the tuxedo. He rolled up the too-long sleeves.

"Let's get on with it, Deena," said Tommy, the man who'd been dragging D.B. "What do we do with these two?"

Deena scratched the scar tracks of her missing eye. She merely glanced at D.B., dismissing the young girl instantly. But Eric she studied hard and with interest. She pulled a pair of pliers out of her back pocket, knelt next to her husband's body, and pried open his mouth. Quickly she worked the pliers in, clamped them on a rear molar, and twisted and yanked until the tooth ripped from his mouth trailing bloody saliva. "Gold caps," she explained to Eric. "Gold still has some value even now." She tossed the tooth to the kid in the tux. He opened a felt Seagrams bag and dropped the tooth in. It clacked against others like a bag of marbles.

"Well?" Tommy said, tugging his leather driving gloves tighter.

"Check their teeth," Deena said.

Tommy prodded Eric's chest with the point of his knife. Eric stared back but didn't budge.

"Open it or I'll cut it open," Tommy said.

Eric opened his mouth. The man probed around with his fingers, peeling back Eric's lips for a better look. "A couple fillings, that's all," he reported to Deena.

"Check the teeny-bopper," Deena said.

The man stood in front of D.B. "Open."

"Fuck yourself," D.B. said.

The man slapped her twice, forehand and backhand. Her face swelled with splotchy red welts.

"That all you got?" D.B. sneered. "I've been hit harder by a heavy rain."

Deena chuckled. "You need help, Tommy?"

Tommy spun around, glared at Deena. Obviously a

candidate for husband number four, Eric thought. Tommy then turned back to D.B. and socked her hard in the jaw, sending her sprawling backward to the ground. She lay there, dazed, her body barely moving. Tommy squatted beside her, forced her mouth open, and checked her teeth.

"One," he said happily.

"Tote that tooth, lift that biscuspid," Deena said.

Tommy jammed his pliers into D.B.'s mouth. He started tugging, lifting D.B.'s sluggish head from the ground.

Eric watched a moment. He looked at Deena, at the others, all rapt in Tommy's actions like hungry wolves watching a rabbit being disemboweled. It would be stupid to try anything against them. Too many. What was one lousy tooth compared with their lives? He had been trained to ignore emotion, he reminded himself. But watching Tommy's gleeful attack on helpless D.B., Eric decided to indulge himself. His movements were swift and sudden, too quick for anyone to stop him.

Eric took three running steps forward, brought his right leg back, and kicked Tommy's jaw as hard as he could. Tommy's head snapped back with a terrible crack, flipping him in a backward arc away from D.B. The pliers flew into the dirt.

A dozen guards quickly thrust their weapons against Eric's chest and back, but Eric had stopped moving anyway. He stood and waited as D.B. struggled to her feet, rubbing her jaw. She winked at Eric. "My hero. Kinda like the tooth fairy in reverse."

The young boy in the white tuxedo squatted over Tommy, listening at his chest. He shook his head. "Not a peep. I think his neck is busted."

Deena sighed. "He couldn't do much right."

"Can I have the gloves," the boy asked, already

tugging them off Tommy's limp hands.

Deena walked up to Eric. "Pretty soon you're going to have made a complete wardrobe for the boy."

"Let us go," Eric said. "We don't want anything from you."

Deena laughed. "But we want something from you." She gestured to the others. "Strip them naked," she commanded.

Dozens of hands began pulling at Eric and D.B.'s clothing.

4

"Not bad," Deena said, staring at Eric's naked body. Her eyes drifted from the thick chest muscles down the narrow waist, the cubed stomach muscles. She lingered on his penis and grinned. "You got a name?"

"You asking me or my penis?"

Deena laughed. "You're funny. It would be a shame to kill you without sampling the goods."

"As long as you share," a bearish bearded man from the crowd said. He stepped forward wearing a high school letter sweater with a hole above the heart. An ancient dark stain ringed the hole. The letter was a large white L with a basketball embedded in it. He tapped a long machete against his thigh. His cold eyes stared into Eric's. "Sharing is the sign of a wise leader, Deena."

"Which do you want, Edgar?" Deena asked him. "Him or her?"

Edgar's smile curled his lips, revealing small yellowed teeth. "Both."

"You're too greedy, Edgar. Always have been."

"Always will be," Edgar chuckled.

Deena said to Eric, "Usually he settles for the bodies we dig up, if they're not too ripe. You can see why it's so tough to find a good husband around here."

"Dating is hard," Eric said.

Deena laughed. "I'm going to hate to lose you."

"But you will. Right?"

She shrugged. "Eventually. Either you try something stupid again and we'll have to kill you. Or we sell you off with her. No offense, but sexy young girls bring a lot more than guys, even guys in your kind of shape. Finally a society that recognizes a woman's true worth."

Eric watched her strut in front of him, reminding everyone who was in charge. Actually she was quite attractive, even with the missing eye and ear. Her face had the lean sharp lines of a model, the angles that all led to her mouth, full and wide and cruel. Her body was long, slim-hipped but not boyish. She wore bib overalls with nothing underneath. The bib part barely covered her large breasts. Hard muscles were layered across the top of her chest and down her arms, hinting at the power beneath. The scars over her eye and ear seemed almost decorative, exotic marks, like beauty spots or punk make-up. Maybe he'd just seen too many scars by now to be affected. Or maybe he had too many of his own.

He stood with his hands at his sides, not wanting to appear afraid or ashamed. The object now was to stay alive. Not just for his sake or D.B.'s, but for Tim. Someone had to steal Tim back from Fallows. And no one else but Eric would be crazy enough to try.

Deena stood in front of him now, barely brushing his body as she reached up and let her finger trace the long scar that started at the base of his neck, sprouted straight up, hung right along the jawbone, edging up over the jaw and ending on his cheek in a white splotch like a burst skyrocket. "Nasty," she said. "How'd it happen?"

"Clipping my toenails. One sliver flew up and sliced me clean open."

Her finger lingered on his face. She leaned close enough now that her hip brushed across his penis. She was trying to arouse him. Humiliate him.

Thing is, Eric thought, it was working. She was sexy and her touch was just right. He could feel himself stirring. He had to concentrate. Control himself. He thought back on Big Bill Tenderwolf, the Hopi Indian who had trained him as a teenager. Big Bill dumping a bag of charcoal on the ground, soaking it in lighter fluid, then tossing in a match. Watching it burn while he sipped his beer.

Eric had sat on the porch not knowing what today's lesson was, but feeling cocky, a little arrogant. "That the way your ancestors did it? Lighter fluid and Quick-Start charcoal?"

Big Bill had just smiled and tossed on more charcoal. When the flames had died down and there was nothing left but fiery red coals, Big Bill had waved Eric over. "Take off your shoes."

"What for?" Eric had said.

Big Bill smiled again. "Gonna teach you a new dance step. The Hopi Hot Foot."

"What?"

"It's all the rage on the reservation. You'll love it."

"Like hell." Eric crossed his arms and shook his head. He'd endured a lot of painful lessons from this man, but this was asking too much.

When Big Bill sighed it was like a hard wind rattling between icy mountains. He sighed now. "Control, Eric. That's what life is all about. There are some things over which you have no control. The weather. The Lakers. Certain situations. The craziness of others. But there are things you can control, manipulate. First and most important, you must be able to control yourself. Physically and mentally. Control your emotions."

"Then you're nothing but a robot," Eric said.

"I didn't say destroy emotions, I said control them. Like a wild stallion. Your emotions are like that stallion, especially at your age. If you try to tie the horse up, cage it in, it will die. And if you let it run free without any control, it will carry you over a cliff. Either way, you will be destroyed." He finished the can of beer and tossed the empty can onto the smoldering coals. A few drops of beer sizzled. "But if you can ride that stallion, learn to make it do what you want, when you want, then you will have the greatest ride of your life. You understand?"

Eric shrugged.

"Good enough. You must start this control by being able to control your emotions. Pain is an emotion."

"Bullshit. Pain is a physical fact. Nerve endings, receptor impulses, and frontal lobes. That stuff."

"True. But it conspires with the imagination to exaggerate the facts." He tapped his temple. "Mind over matter. Love, hate, fear, and desire. The person who controls those four emotions cannot be controlled by anyone else. Now, what you're going to do is walk slowly across those hot coals with your bare feet—"

"No way!"

"It's easy. Concentrate. Empty your mind of the concept of pain. Imagine the hot coals are ice cubes, cool to the touch on this hot day. Your feet welcome them. You must—" He frowned. "You're not concentrating."

"Damn straight. I'm not going to do it."

"Hopi children do this. It's like hopscotch for them."

"Fine. I'll watch."

Big Bill sighed again, deep gusts of disappointment blowing past Eric. "Oh hell, I'll do it myself." He tugged off his fancy snakeskin boots and socks. Stood at the edge of the bright coals. He closed his eyes, slowed his breathing down.

He took his first step.

Eric watched Big Bill's face. There was no sign of pain, no hesitation, no hollering. Just a little tightening of skin around the mouth and eyes. A few drops of sweat on the tip of his hawk-nose. Big Bill took another step, the bare soles of his feet hushing against the glowing coals. Still no reaction. Three more steps and he was through it. He opened his eyes and stared at Eric. He wiped the sweat from his nose and smiled. "See? Like I said, easy."

Eric nodded, indeed impressed. But no closer to actually doing it himself.

"Think it over," Big Bill said, walking toward his house. "I'll get another beer and be right back."

Eric watched him walk away, his steps sure and hard, as if he had only walked on ice cubes. Amazing.

So amazing, Eric decided to follow him, just to make sure. He crept around the side of the house and peered in through the kitchen window over the sink. He saw Big Bill limping gingerly to the chair, two trays of ice cubes in one hand and a fat jar of aloe vera salve in the other. He sat at the kitchen table, his face wincing from pain. Under each foot he placed an ice cube tray. He alternately cursed his own

31

stupidity and praised the miracle of ice. Then he rubbed the aloe vera salve into the soles of his feet. Eric couldn't see them, but he could imagine the size those burn blisters must be.

Eric hurried back to the coals. It wouldn't do for Big Bill to be caught in his lie and embarrassed. Eric felt terrible thinking of the pain and suffering his Indian friend had endured just to teach Eric. He knew firewalking was common among many of the Indians, so it was possible. He didn't doubt Big Bill had done it when he was younger. But that was long ago. Eric felt bad. He couldn't let Big Bill down, not now.

He kicked off his penny loafers and removed his socks. He regulated his breathing, concentrating on the rhythm, not the amount of air. Feeling the air at the bottom of his lungs, not just the tops. He emptied his mind of fear. Thought about the worst pain possible and how silly pain was anyway. Just impulses flickering along a thread like nerve. Nothing to it.

He stepped onto the coals.

And felt—

—what?—

—nothing.

Not any temperature. Not heat. Not coolness. Barely the pressure of anything at all, almost as if he walked on air. The rest of the steps were the same.

He was several steps past the coals when he realized he'd done it. There was that little difference. He immediately sat on the ground and examined his soles. No blisters. Not even red.

Applause.

Big Bill Tenderwolf leaned against the porch, an open can of beer pinned between arm and chest, applauding with both hands. "Very good, Eric."

"You showed me how."

"Ah, yes. I did, didn't I. But not in the way you think." He reached into his pocket and pulled out a can of Coke and tossed it to Eric. "You watched me in the kitchen, didn't you? Saw me with the ice and salve?"

Eric hesitated. "Yes."

Big Bill laughed, showed Eric the soles of his feet. No blisters. "That's what I mean by control, Eric. No way were you going to walk those coals, I knew that. Unless I could control you. How? By using your guilt, challenging your sense of accomplishment. You couldn't resist doing something I failed at. Beating me just once, even if I never knew. Right?"

"No, I . . ." Eric stopped, nodded. "Right."

"*That's* control. Making your body do what you want; making other bodies do what you want."

Now Eric stood stark naked surrounded by a gang of graverobbers, the one-eyed, one-eared female leader rubbing up against him. And he willed his body not to respond.

It didn't.

Deena stood back, stared at his penis with surprise. "Either you are a very disciplined man or you're more interested in Edgar than you are in me. Which is it?"

"Neither," D.B. piped in. "He's my man."

Eric almost smiled, except for D.B.'s earnestness. True, she'd tried seducing him periodically over the past few months, and true, he'd been tempted to give in. Still, something of the old civilization still remained within him and he'd avoided bedding the eighteen-year-old girl. Watching her stand there, unashamedly naked, hands defiantly on her slender hips as she yelled into Deena's face, Eric felt proud of her.

Deena laughed. "My dear, no one is anyone's anymore. By tomorrow morning you'll have been everyone's in this camp. You won't be able to remember the last dozen men who fucked you or what end they did it to. And when you're able to walk again, we'll sell you to someone who'll do the same thing."

"That doesn't scare me," D.B. said. And Eric could see that it didn't. She'd had all that happen to her before. She'd been more afraid of walking through the cemetery, the primal childhood fears. This grim reality was only what she'd expected. She fingered her choke collar, the only thing still on her naked body.

"What are we waiting for," Edgar said. "Let's tie them up and do them now. It'll be light soon." He grabbed a hunk of rope from one of the guards and gestured to Eric. "Turn around."

Eric didn't move. He looked around, studying every possibility. His crossbow and bolts were being held by a skinny middle-aged man over by the open grave. D.B.'s gun was empty and they had no more bullets in their backpacks. The backpacks had already been emptied and the food and clothing inside distributed to the scavengers around them. Escape did not look possible.

He would try anyway. Because he knew one thing about himself: he knew that he was going to kill this man Edgar. Control was one thing, but Eric knew there are some things he would not submit to. This was one. He would kill Edgar and they would try to kill him. Their ambivalence toward death was not unusual considering their surroundings, but they'd only let him live after having killed several of their men because they could still make a profit selling him. One more killing and Eric was no longer cost-effective.

There had to be a way out. A man who can walk on fire can cross any threshold, that's what Big Bill Tenderwolf had told him. But how? He was surrounded by twenty armed animals.

"You're lucky," Eric stalled. "All these rotting bodies. I'm surprised you haven't caught any diseases."

"Shut up and turn around," Edgar said, looping his rope.

"Oh we have," Deena said, cutting Edgar off. "There were many more of us before. Some had come up from Lake Elsinore, most had filtered down from Mission Viejo."

"We passed through Mission Viejo yesterday. Not much left."

"Yeah, well it was one of those planned communities. You've seen their slogan on billboards: The California Promise. They planned everything but the fucking earthquake that ripped through there. I ought to know; I was one of their planners." She laughed. "That's right. Used to plan where to put all those wonderful plants you see everywhere. All day with blueprints deciding whether to use pyracantha or jacaranda or maybe gazania. Now I just decide who lives and who dies."

"And this is more fun," Eric said.

"Yeah, it is." She smiled. "Hard to believe a nice WASP college girl like me would be doing this, huh? From Yuppie Princess to the Pirate Queen of Graverobbers. Okay, maybe it stinks. But I'll tell you something, it beats taking shit from a bunch of macho assholes who acted like they were gods because they let me work for them. If you ever get to the outside world again, go ask any professional woman if she wouldn't trade places with me. See how long it takes her to answer."

"He's stalling, goddamn it," Edgar said.

"Of course he is," Deena said. "So what? He's not going anywhere. You'll get your share of him." She shook her head at Eric. "You know, that's the one bad thing about this surviving. It's fucking boring. I mean, we eat and dig up graves and fuck. That's it. Edgar here was a pool cleaner for Mission Viejo so you can imagine what fun he is to talk to. The most fun we have is guessing what the corpse we dig up will be wearing."

"What do you eat?" Eric asked.

"Before I got here, they were eating the bodies. That's why a lot of them died."

Eric nodded. "Embalming fluid."

"Right. Now we leave some of the fresh bodies we kill lying at the bottom of an open grave. That brings the coyotes and dogs from the hills. Then we pop out of our hiding places, kill them, and eat them. Not as easy as it sounds." She pointed to her missing eye and ear. "One wild coyote was still alive. Jumped at me before I managed to get my knife in his throat. He did a little damage."

"What happens to the people who wander through here?"

"Kill them or sell them."

"Pretty tidy," Eric said. "You must have been a good planner."

"Take a look." She swept her hands out to encompass the whole cemetery. "This is my better mouse-trap."

"Just one question," Eric said. "Why the gold?

What can you possibly do with gold now?"

"Sell it."

"Where? Nobody cares about that anymore."

"Somebody does. And he pays in goods and drugs and whatever else we need."

"Who?"

"A guy has an outpost set up down around San Diego. Has his own damn army and, man, they don't fuck around. Some kind of ex-marine or something. Colonel Dirk Fallows."

Eric's body tensed. The muscles in his stomach and chest rippled like a strong tide. He felt his skin contract all the way up through his scalp. He knew now he was going to make his move. And he knew how.

Edgar shoved him. "Turn around, asshole. It's party time." He nodded to the young kid with the white tux and spear. "He tries anything, Dean, stick him."

"You bet," Dean said. He jabbed his spear up against Eric's stomach.

Edgar looped the rope around one wrist first. "Guess we'll start with you face down. This is the way we did it in prison. Yeah, I done time. Some burglary. Used to check out the houses with pools then hit them later."

Eric felt the rope tighten around his right wrist, the rough hemp pinching his skin. His arm shoved painfully up between his shoulder blades. If he didn't do something before Edgar tied the left wrist, it would be too late.

Eric moved.

A slight movement at first. Hardly noticeable. Except to Edgar, who saw Eric's right hand coming back down. Edgar grabbed the hand with both of his, but Eric's strength was too great. The slabs of muscles across his back flexed and the hand came down. Now Eric was turning, just a little, grabbing with his right hand the rope that led to his wrist, wrapping it around Edgar's forearm, and jerking hard.

"Shit!" Edgar yelled.

Eric felt Dean's spear pressing into his stomach, the skin breaking. But it was all happening so slowly, so clearly, he knew he had plenty of time. Even as he felt the brass letter opener digging into his stomach, he yanked on the rope, swung Edgar around, and plowed him straight into Dean, knocking the boy to the ground.

"The spear," he said to D.B. and she dove for it. She snatched it away from the boy.

Now everyone else was moving. The skinny man with Eric's crossbow was struggling to cock it. The others behind Eric were lifting their clubs and swords and spears and coming toward him.

Deena drew out her own machete and raised it over her head.

Eric flicked his wrist and the rope around Edgar's wrist unwound. An instant later, just as Edgar was rising to one knee rubbing his skinned wrist, Eric whipped the rope around Edgar's neck. Edgar grabbed at the rope, trying to uncoil it. But suddenly he was being lifted off the ground.

Eric held the rope with both hands now and was swinging Edgar around as if practicing a hammer throw. Edgar clawed frantically at the rope as he swung through the air, his feet smacking into the charging graverobbers, knocking them over as they got closer.

D.B. crouched by Eric's legs. Edgar's orbiting

body whooshed over her head.

Edgar's face was reddish blue. He dug his fingers under the rope, but the momentum kept the rope tight. He gasped for air, but none squeezed under the rope.

"Now what, King Kong?" D.B. asked. She jabbed the spear out at any feet that came close.

"We move," Eric said. Slowly he staggered forward, still swinging Edgar like a propeller. He walked carefully toward the skinny man who was still trying to cock the crossbow.

A sallow man in his mid-twenties prodded Eric with a pitchfork. Eric stepped toward him and swung Edgar at him. The man dodged back, jabbed again. The tines of the pitchfork stuck Edgar's calf. Edgar gurgled hoarsely.

"Come on," Deena commanded her followers. "All at once." She stalked toward Eric, her machete high over her head. Sweat gathered in the socket of her missing eye. The moisture glistened off the scar tissue. In the orange glow of the lantern it looked like a real eye. "You know," she said to Eric, "now we'll have to kill you."

Eric watched them form a half-circle, closing in on him. Behind him the open grave yawned. He glanced down, winced at what he saw.

It looked like a butcher's shop. Arms, hands, legs, torsos. All jumbled together like spare parts, but not connected to anything. And on top, a dead German shepherd and a golden retriever, each with a spear through his chest. They'd thrown the body parts in as bait to lure the dogs, then killed the dogs for food. The better mousetrap, Deena had said.

The smell sent a surge of bitter bile up Eric's throat. He swallowed hard.

"D.B.?" Eric said.

"What?" She was still hunched over Edgar's swinging body, stabbing her spear at kneecaps.

Eric nodded at the skinny man fumbling with his crossbow. "Him."

"Right."

"When I tell you."

Deena's machete sliced air close to Eric's chest. She jumped back again as Edgar came hurtling around. The long blade whacked into Edgar's shin, slicing open a long nasty gash. He could only manage a choked gasp. Deena didn't care. Eric could see her face was determined, she would get him now even if she had to chop Edgar up piece by piece.

"Now!" Eric yelled. D.B. rolled out from under Edgar and charged straight at the skinny man. He brought the crossbow up as a shield, but too late. She rammed her spear into his chest, knocking him into the open grave with the body parts and dead dogs. D.B. grabbed the metal crossbow and quiver of bolts. She hesitated.

"Run, damn it," Eric shouted. "Run!"

She did. Her pale naked body seemed almost iridescent under the eerie glow of the Long Beach Halo. He glanced over his shoulder, saw her disappearing into the darkness, and turned his attention back to the graverobbers.

Deena swung the machete again at him, this time hacking into Edgar's ankle, nearly severing the foot. The sneakered foot hung by a knot of tendon and bone. Edgar didn't mind. He had strangled to death twenty seconds earlier.

Eric kept swinging the body around and around over his head. Part of him wanted to laugh: he pictured himself, naked, swinging a corpse over his head like Steve Reeves in those Italian muscleman movies he'd loved as a kid. Absurd. But part of him wanted to kill: stay here and battle until each of these graverobbers was dead. His hatred was fierce, a physical heat that burned up his spine like napalm. He had to kill them or be consumed by his own fire.

Also absurd.

He was out of control. Big Bill Tenderwolf had warned him against the bloodlust. "Use hate, Eric," Bill had said. "It can be a good ally. But when it becomes so strong you do stupid things to satisfy it, then it's your enemy. It will get you killed."

That's what would happen here, Eric realized. There was no way he could defeat all of them. Deena's own bloodlust was clouding her thinking, but she was smart. Soon she would calm down and organize her gang into a better formation.

Eric released the rope.

Edgar's body flip-flopped through the air, arms and legs splayed. He thumped into Deena and two other gang members, knocking them all down.

Eric ran. The night air cooled his skin. The fire along his spine was extinguished. He ran silently, bare feet barely grazing the ground before launching back into the air. He leapt broken tombstones, open graves, as if some automatic sense had kicked in. His twisted ankle didn't even hurt. The running felt good.

"Over there!" Deena said. Heavy footsteps clomped behind Eric.

D.B. sprang out from behind a gravestone and fell in beside Eric. She was an excellent sprinter, matching Eric's pace fairly well. However, he knew she wouldn't be able to keep it up for long.

"Why'd you stop?" he asked.

41

"Wait . . . for . . . you," she panted. She handed him the crossbow as they ran. It was cocked and loaded.

"Not bad."

"I'm stronger . . . than I . . . look."

"Keep running," Eric said. He stopped suddenly, turned, aimed at the dark figures running toward him. Even in the dark he could tell which was Deena; the machete tight in her hand, the pony tail flipping side to side as she ran. He aimed the crossbow at her, his eye looking down the length of the bolt, lining up the sharp tip with her chest.

He swung the crossbow to her left and aimed at another figure. He couldn't tell if it was male or female, only that it carried a rake. Eric fired and the bolt whizzed through the dark. The figure dropped to the ground.

Deena and the others kept coming.

Eric stood, turned, saw D.B. still standing there, staring at him. "I told you to keep running."

She didn't say anything. She fell back into pace, running alongside him. He could feel her unasked question: Why didn't you shoot her?

Nothing was said. They kept running. D.B. began to fall behind and Eric hooked an arm around her waist and kept her moving. He looked down and saw blood coming from her left foot. She'd stepped on something sharp but hadn't mentioned it. He didn't either.

Soon the graverobbers began to drop away, exhausted. They didn't have the stamina. Digging up graves all day wasn't much training for running.

Only Deena was still chasing them and even she had dropped way behind. Then she stopped too.

Eric waited, listening. He could hear Deena's loud

panting, gasping for air. They had left the graveyard two miles ago. Now they were standing in a small patch of woods. A few abandoned bulldozers were scattered about. They had been in the process of clearing the trees for another housing project. Wishing Well Springs, according to the signs. A planned community.

"Okay, okay," Deena yelled. She paused, still breathing heavily. "You've made it. But you ever come back here again, I'll have your balls. And that," she said, "is the California Promise."

Eric and D.B. watched her turn and walk away.

Eric looked at D.B. "Well, ask and get it over with."

5

"It's almost ready," Eric said, leaning over the fire.

"Hmmm," D.B. said. "Cute buns."

Eric straightened up, embarrassed.

D.B. laughed. "Some Warlord. Blushes at the slightest compliment."

Eric stirred the concoction bubbling on the fire. "Keep your mind on what you're doing."

"Hey, you're the Calvin Klein who designed these things. I can't help it they're so revealing."

"We didn't have much material to work with."

"So you say." She giggled.

He gave her a stern look, but she just laughed. He knew she was teasing him and he went along with it. It was nice to have her back to her old self, joking and singing, endlessly quoting song lyrics. Last night after Deena had turned back he'd expected D.B. to ask him why he hadn't killed her. But she hadn't. She ignored him, not in a sulky way, but more in a thoughtful way, as if she were wrestling with some internal confusion.

They'd spent the night exploring the woods. Over in the clearing they'd found the three rusted bulldozers, the gasoline long syphoned out of each. A t-shirt had been tied to the back of one of the seats and a dented hardhat lay nearby. Eric had taken the hardhat, the t-shirt, and stripped one of the seats of its vinyl covering.

The t-shirt was filthy, yellowed under the arms from old sweat. Across the chest it read: *I don't swim in your toilet, don't you piss in my pool.* Eric had cut the t-shirt into two loinclothes and a halter top. Despite the t-shirt being an extra-large, there wasn't much material for all three garments, so all were a little skimpy. "Looks like a coupla jock straps," D.B. had decided. Eric agreed. The halter top had been a concession to modesty rather than need. D.B.'s breasts were small and firm enough not to need support, but Eric's resolve to maintain a fatherly relationship with her was hard enough as it was.

The hardhat was on the fire now, cooking some of the sap he'd gathered from a few pine trees. He could smell the turpentine evaporating as he stirred the thick resin left behind.

"Is it soup yet?" D.B. said, sniffing the fumes. She held the pieces of vinyl seat she'd been cutting with a sharp rock.

"It won't harden until I add some wood ashes," Eric said. He threw a fistful into the hardhat.

"So, Colonel Sanders, that's your secret recipe."

Eric removed the hardhat from the fire. He kept stirring. "Okay, get ready."

D.B. stood, each foot planted on a hunk of vinyl. Carefully she wrapped one piece around her foot into a crude moccasin. Eric dipped the stick from the hardhat onto the vinyl, gluing the flaps down. They repeated the process with the other foot.

"Now hold it in place until I say otherwise."

D.B. stooped, pressing the flaps together with the heels of her palms. "So this is how you like your women, squatting at your feet."

"Right. That and at least ten years older."

45

"Bullshit. I can see you like me. Remember Gary Puckett and the Union Gap? 'Young girl, get out of my mind/My love for you is way out of line.' Or the Lovin' Spoonful. 'Younger girl keeps a roamin' through my mind/No matter how much I try I can't seem to leave my troubles behind.' See? Musical history backs me up. I rest my case."

"Good. Now rest your mouth."

She laughed. "You're so easy to tease."

"How's the foot?"

She flexed it. "Not bad. The swelling's gone down. How's the shoulder?"

He shrugged it. The spear wound and the bite had been superficial. "I might not play power forward for the Lakers this season."

She looked up at him. "I guess it's San Diego next, huh?"

"They don't have a basketball team."

She frowned, gave him a serious look. "You know what I mean."

"That's where Fallows is and that's where Tim is. So that's where I go."

"There you go again. It's always 'I.' Why don't you say 'we,' as in 'we go'?"

"Because it's dangerous. You don't have to go, I do."

She shook her head as if he were a slow student unable to grasp a simple lesson. "Forget it. Change of subject. What Deena said about Fallows. Why would he be buying gold? What good is gold or any of that junk in California?"

"I don't know. I just want Tim."

She put her glasses on and looked up at the sky. The sun was a long orange smear behind the Long Beach Halo, giving a yellow-orange tint to the sky. "It's so pretty, hard to believe it's poison."

Eric barely heard her. He was already thinking of Dirk Fallows and Tim. It had been over a year since the quakes. Nine months since Tim's capture. Eighty-four days since Tim's thirteenth birthday. The last time Eric had seen him he had grown a couple inches, had filled out some. But more important, he had changed inside. Just a little, but in the wrong direction. Dirk Fallows was a master of psychological conditioning. Brainwashing. Eric had seen him turn Cong prisoners around until they didn't know what was right or wrong, only that Dirk Fallows was their god. Eric woke every day knowing that Tim was another day further from him and closer to Fallows.

D.B. was speaking to him. "That was some trick you pulled off last night, John Wayning it through the graveyard, knocking them around with that guy's body swinging over your head. Ought to be an Olympic event. Hey, maybe we'll have our own California Olympics soon. Nifty events like Power Gravedigging, Corpse Tossing, Teeth Yanking. Go for the gold."

"I doubt whether most of them will be alive six months from now."

"What?"

"You notice how pale and sickly they looked?"

She shrugged. "It was tough to tell in the dark. Deena looked pretty healthy." She held her hands out from her chest to indicate the size of Deena's breasts.

"She's smarter than the others, more careful. They've been eating those dogs, sometimes after they've already been feeding off those older half-rotten corpses."

"So?"

"A lot of those bodies are filled with embalming fluid. Once the dog ingests it, so will the people. That's not too healthy."

47

She made a disgusted face. "Jeez. That's gross."

Eric shrugged.

D.B. watched him for a minute before speaking. "That why you didn't kill Deena? You figured she'd die anyway?"

Eric didn't answer.

"I know it's not because she's a woman. You don't discriminate in life, you sure don't in death. And I know it's not because of her missing eye or ear. Hell, we run into that shit all the time. Besides, she still managed to look like a knockout. So what was it?"

"The Civil War," Eric said.

"Huh?"

"That's when embalming became popular. Up until then, most people thought it was like mutilating a body. But after the war, the government had so many bodies to ship home they awarded contracts to embalmers so the corpses would be somewhat preserved on the trip." Eric tossed a log on the dying fire. "Actually, embalming started a century earlier. There's a famous case of Mrs. Martin Van Butcell, in 1775, whose will specified that her husband could keep control of her fortune only as long as her body remained above ground. The husband had her embalmed and placed in a glass-lidded case in a sitting room. He even held visiting hours."

"You're stalling me just like you stalled them last night."

"I'm talking about death. What it means to different people. In Borneo, the dead were often kept among the living while the body decomposed. They were even given food and water. The Indonesians used to attach mystical importance to the body's disintegration, carefully collecting the liquids produced by decomposition and later mixing them with rice and eating the rice."

"Tell it to Uncle Ben." She stood up, tested the moccasins. The glue held. "I don't think I want to hear anymore."

"Okay." He dumped the rest of the glue from the hardhat. There hadn't been enough vinyl for a second pair of moccasins.

D.B. walked over and stood in front of him. Eric had made the halter so the word *don't* was visible over her left breast. She'd laughed when she'd put it on and kissed him on the cheek. There was no smile on her face now. "I lied," she said. "I want to hear more. I like it when you act like a teacher."

Eric smiled.

"I just hope you were clearer in the classroom than you are now."

"I'll try," he said. "The point is, as a civilized people we make up rules, standards to live by. But those rules depend on need. Even concerning death, the one thing all people have in common, all people hold in awe. In some South American and European countries where space is relatively scarce, people often lease graves. Then after three or five years, the bodies are exhumed and the bones stuck in a communal grave."

"Lease, huh? Not even an option to buy?"

"You see how that concept would be disgusting to some people? Or the Zoroastrians, who thought the human body so unclean that to bury it would contaminate the pure elements of the earth."

D.B. looked into Eric's eyes. "You saying that what those graverobbers were doing wasn't wrong?"

"Capturing us was wrong. Wanting to sell us was wrong. The rest was survival."

"I knew it," D.B. said. "Last night I thought about it. 'Why didn't Doc Rock kill her?' I asked myself. 'Why didn't he shoot that one-eyed, one-horned flying purple people-eater?' I thought about it the whole night, even when we were out exploring."

"Did you reach a conclusion?"

"At first I thought it was 'cause she was a looker. Even you must get horny sometimes. But nope, that didn't figure. You could have had me any time you wanted. It had to be something else. Then it hit me. You looked at her and you saw yourself. Not what you are, but what you're becoming. Or at least afraid of becoming."

Eric threw another log on the fire. "Gold star."

"I'm not dumb just because I'm a kid, you know."

"I know."

"I mean, I'm a singer, an artist. I'm sensitive to people. Like I know how hard you have to get to keep going after this Fallows guy. How you have to guard against becoming the same kind of guy he is. If you get to be just like him, then what good will it do Tim to rescue him. Right?" She turned away, kicked some dirt into the fire. "I tease you, but I know why you won't sleep with me, even though I can tell there are times you want to. There's a line you've drawn between what you have to do to survive, to get Tim back, and what you have to do to remain civilized, whatever that means. I'm part of that line. Touching a kid would be wrong and eighteen is still a kid. To you."

Eric reached out both hands and grasped her shoulders, turning her to face him. Her eyes brimmed with tears. "Not as much as before."

"Yeah, we'll see."

Eric glanced up at the Long Beach Halo. D.B.'s insight had surprised him. But she had not gone far enough, not recognized how far he had already gone toward being like Deena. Like Fallows. There had been many, many nights he had considered sneaking off in the darkness and leaving D.B. behind. This quest of revenge and rescue was no place for her, he'd rationalized, knowing all along that if he left her, her chances of survival were greatly reduced. And sometimes not caring. There were times, in fact, when he wasn't sure if he wanted Fallows more for revenge than to free Tim.

There were different kinds of survival. Survival of the body. But of what use was that if the person you had spent your whole life becoming was lost in the process. That was a kind of suicide.

Seeing Deena panting after them last night, her one missing eye sealed over with scars like rubber zippers, her missing ear a puckered hole, she had seemed like a new species of animal. Attractive, yet marked. Her life of amorality had made him want to run to her. Sign up for the program. And that moment made Eric afraid. Had he pulled his trigger then, it would have been for the wrong reason: because of what she represented to him, what he feared in himself. He'd had to let her live, to prove when confronted with such choices, he could still make the right decision.

So far.

Eric picked up his crossbow and slung the quiver of bolts across his chest. "Let's see if we can scavenge some better clothing than this before it cools down tonight."

"Actually," D.B. said lightly, "what we're wearing looks a lot like what fashionable couples wear on the French Riviera. Not that I've been there, but I've seen pictures in *Cosmopolitan*."

She chatted on as they hiked, discussing certain singers she liked or didn't like, talking about her record collection, which before the quakes had occupied two entire walls of her bedroom, but after the quakes had occupied five 33-gallon garbage cans. Eric, as usual, was quiet, responding rarely. He found some prickly pears, peeled the sharp spines, and fed them both. He spotted some fresh rabbit tracks and traced them to a small pond. He filled the vinyl bag he'd made from the leftover seatcover with water.

They stayed away from any signs of people.

That night Eric made camp. While D.B. gathered firewood, he scouted ahead. A mile away he found a wide shallow grave. He dug up the bodies. Two women and four men were buried. The two women and three of the men had been shot. One man was dressed in camouflage fatigues and had a hole through his chest that looked like it had been made by an arrow. The bodies were almost completely decomposed.

Eric stared. The name stitched into the shirt of the fatigues was *Driscol*. Eric remembered the name, remembered the uniform.

It was the last time he'd seen Tim. Tim running toward Eric, gathering speed to leap the ravine and escape Fallows. Fallows squinting down the sights of his Walther at Tim. Firing. Tim's leg kicking out from under him. Three of Fallows armed men rushing to his side, forcing Eric to flee. Fallows shouting, "He's mine, Eric. My son now!" Eric diving for cover as the three men opened fire. But Fallows had called them each by name: Leyson, Rendall, Driscol.

Driscol.

It wasn't hard to figure out. Fallows and his men had swept through here on their way to San Diego, found some people they could loot. Some ran, others fought. Those that fought died. But not before killing Driscol.

Eric stripped Driscol's clothing off and those of

the thinnest woman. He put Driscol's clothes on, though they were tight around Eric's muscular chest and arms. He returned to the camp where he'd left D.B. and tossed her the jeans and turtleneck sweater.

She didn't ask where they'd come from. She just put them on.

She was learning.

6

The leaflets fluttered down from the sky.

"Here they come again," D.B. said.

Eric shaded his eyes with his hand and looked up. The yellow leaflets drifted out of the cloudy thickness of the Long Beach Halo like some kind of snow flurry. If it weren't for the faint buzz of the unseen planes above the Halo, it might seem as if some giant pillow in the sky had burst and these were the golden feathers spinning down to earth. The makings of fables, Eric thought. In the beginning, there were leaflets . . .

D.B. put her glasses on and ran to catch one as it swayed back and forth in the air, tossed by wind currents. She ran back and forth under it, arms reaching up, too impatient to wait for it to touch the ground.

Eric sat on the ground and waited. During the first months after the disaster, the U.S. government had dropped them once a week, then every month. Now they came sporadically, lumping together the news of the world during the past several months into half a page of brief updates. They always contained half a page of assurances at how hard the government was working to reverse the Long Beach Halo and rescue those still stranded on California. It also always contained bright red cautions about not trying to leave the island until they've completed their medical research on the effects. Anyone trying to pass through to the outside world, they warned, would be immediately terminated.

At first, Eric had looked forward to the leaflets, rereading them over and over, looking for some sign of hope that the nightmare might soon be over. Order restored. But the encouraging words soon sounded hollow. The rhetoric about rescue, scientific research, the call for patience, faith, patriotism, all became just so much nonsense. Eric soon realized they weren't ever going to do anything. The cost was too great to justify in Congress, the fear too great from the rest of the world. What kind of freaks would emerge to contaminate them?

"Gotcha!" D.B. said, snatching a leaflet from the air. It was one sheet folded into thirds and stapled together. Like an advertisement for a new Chinese restaurant. She slid her thumbnail under the staple and pried it loose. She unfolded the sheet as carefully and with as much anticipation as if she'd just discovered an ancient treasure map. While she eagerly read, Eric watched the enthusiasm drain from her face and sag into disappointment. She crumpled the leaflet and threw it to the ground. Another one fluttered down near her and she slapped it away with her backhand.

"Well?" Eric said.

"It ain't Lucy in the Sky with Diamonds," she said bitterly. "More like Litter from the Sky with Diarrhea."

"Rescue imminent?"

"Right. Any day now. Just have patience."

"And don't leave the island."

"Or *zap,* you're terminated." She fingered her

choke collar. "Think they'll ever get us out of here? Or get rid of the Halo?"

"Sure," Eric said. "Any day now."

"I'm serious." She looked at him, forehead scrunched together in concentration, bunching all her freckles into a swarm. "Will it ever be like it was?"

"Yes," Eric lied. "It will."

"I never know whether to believe you or not."

"Have I ever lied to you?"

"I can't tell."

He stood up. "Let's get going. Another couple of hours and we'll be in San Diego."

"Swell." She kicked aside a couple of leaflets and walked beside him.

They'd traveled mostly inland, avoiding the beach areas. Despite the tidal waves that had drowned the beach towns of Laguna, San Clemente, Oceanside, and all the others along the coast, crowds of people had returned to the beaches for the fishing. There were always crowds camped there, sleeping in their homemade boats, fighting off the pirates and scavengers.

Instead they'd come out of the Cleveland National forest and hiked south near San Juan Capistrano.

"Think the swallows will return here?" D.B. had asked as they'd walked by the outskirts of town.

"Yeah," Eric had replied. "Only the people here will be waiting for them with knives and forks."

They'd gone further inland, around Camp Pendleton, the old marine base. There was no telling who would be there now. Finally they'd traced the 15 freeway past Escondido, veered east along the 163, then headed south with the 5. That took them to the edge of San Diego.

"You hungry?" Eric asked.

"Depends."

"On what?"

"On whether your remedy is more of those dumb prickly pears or bulrishes or insects."

"What do you want?"

"Meat! I'll eat it raw, cooked, I don't care. I'm starting to feel like some carnivorous cavewoman."

Eric laughed. "We haven't seen much game in the past couple of days. I think they've been scared away, or killed off."

"Please, Eric. Shoot an arrow in the air and maybe it'll hit a bird. I'll Kentucky Fry it myself, I swear."

Eric looked out over the rubble of San Diego. Saw the ocean swirling around a few highrise buildings. "There is one place. Maybe."

"Really? Fresh meat?"

"Maybe. There's a chance that survivors were too afraid to risk going after them. If so, there should be plenty of meat."

"Great. Where?"

Eric smiled. "The San Diego Zoo."

"I feel funny," D.B. said.

"Why?"

"I don't know. The zoo, I guess."

Eric looked at her. "You don't like animals?"

"No, it's not that. My parents used to bring me here as a kid. We'd walk around in the sun all day, point at the animals, eat ice cream at the snack stands. Then, as a treat, we'd stop in at the gift shop and they'd buy me a t-shirt with a panda on it or something else neat."

"You rather not go?"

D.B. shook her head. "No. Just that I'll feel funny eating the animals. Kinda like eating Bambi."

"Maybe we'll get lucky. Eat Mr. Ed instead."

"Mr. Ed? Who's that?"

Eric laughed to himself. "Come on. It's dark enough now." He walked cautiously down the middle of the street, his crossbow cocked and ready. He thumbed the safety off.

In the dark, the middle-class houses that lined the streets leading to the zoo looked like piles of burned firewood. That's all most of them were now. What the earthquakes hadn't ripped apart, the ensuing fires had destroyed. Gas mains ruptured. Explosions followed. Whole cities and forests were wiped out.

As with most of the oceanside cities, the ocean had swept in to reclaim some of the land. At least half a mile of San Diego was under fifty feet of water, the tops of buildings poking out of the ocean surface like ice cubes in a cold drink. The water itself was scummy, sprinkled with floating debris, animal and human carcasses, an airtight VW bug.

They had seen some fires in the city and avoided those neighborhoods. Neighborhoods like these that had been burned out and picked over offered little protection for anybody, so no one stayed here. Still, Eric was careful. He didn't want to get caught as he had in the cemetery.

D.B. had her own weapon, one she'd fashioned herself back at the camp when Eric had tossed her those clothes. One of the garments was a large bra, a 38 C.

D.B. had held it up to her own small chest and grinned. "You've got to be kidding, right?"

"Remember that slingshot you'd made from your last bra?"

"The one the ghoulies in the boneyard got. Hey, good idea."

She used the elastic panels to make another one.

Now she carried the Huck Finn-style slingshot tucked in the waistband of her jeans and a handful of rocks in her pocket. Since then she was always on the lookout for the perfect-sized stones.

"There's one," she said. She stooped over and picked a stone from the street. "It's gotta be just right. The size of an eyeball."

Eric ignored her and kept walking. She scampered up behind him. They continued down a few more dark and gloomy streets. Nothing happened.

Eric tried to keep to the dark shadows. The moon was a little brighter tonight than usual. It lit a whole section of Halo, making it glow smoky white like the fog in old Sherlock Holmes movies.

"There," Eric said. They stopped to look at the entranceway of the zoo.

D.B. sang in a whisper, " 'Someone told me it's all happening at the zoo.' Think this is what Simon & Garfunkel had in mind?"

Eric crept ahead, staying along the wall. The large parking lot to their left was about a quarter full with cars, though most of the cars had been trashed and gutted. Stray bones were scattered about the lot.

"Animal or human?" D.B. asked. Her voice was no longer glib.

"Too dark to tell."

She looked at the wall next to them. "Looks like they've added a few touches since last time I was here."

Eric nodded. The walls, not all that difficult to scale, had been topped with barbed wire and broken glass. Trip wires were woven into the barbed wire so that any disturbance would rattle the bells strung along the wall. Primitive, but effective. "At least we know someone is in there."

"But we don't know how many? Maybe a whole

gang is in there slowly feeding off the animals."

Eric raised an eyebrow. "Prickly pears anyone?"

D.B. sighed. "Let's go."

It didn't take Eric long to climb the wall and silence the bells. He threw his shirt over the barbed wire and hoisted D.B. up. She stepped over the wire and hopped down to the other side. Eric put his shirt on and jumped down too.

"Lookit," D.B. said, pointing excitedly. Three grayish flamingos stood by the water's edge, their faces buried under their wings. "How come they're not pink? They were pink last time I was here."

"They're only pink because they add red dye to their diets. In the wild they eat crustaceans every day so they can stay pink. That's too expensive for a zoo."

"Red die! Shit, how disillusioning." She shook her head at Eric. "How do you know that's true?"

"Okay, it's not true." He walked off.

She ran after him. One flamingo shivered, but otherwise didn't move. "All right, I know you're right. You're always fucking right." She sighed. "Sometimes I get tired of everything you know. It's not like you show off or anything, it's just *so much stuff*. I don't think it's healthy."

Eric kept walking.

"Listen, huh? I'm not saying this right I guess. It's just that some of the junk you know is neat, like how to find water and make things out of plants, that sorta stuff. Important survival stuff. But other stuff, like history guys and, and . . ."

"How flamingos get pink?"

"Right. What the hell good is that anyway?"

Eric could feel her confusion and anger. He stopped and stared at her a moment. He'd seen that reaction before, heard almost the exact words every semester, always from one student in each class. Someone who didn't think memorizing a lot of dead people's names and dates had anything to do with them, with whether or not they were popular, got a car, a job, laid. Ironically, it usually wasn't the lazy students who asked the question, but the smart ones. That's why Eric always took the question seriously. Still, this wasn't a classroom. And they probably weren't alone. "Maybe this isn't the time to talk about it."

"Yeah, right. We might get charged by rampaging flamingos."

Wild birds chattered in the dark.

Eric looked her in the eyes. "What do you know most about?"

"Songs. I know more song lyrics than anyone in the world. Go ahead, name a song, any song."

"I believe you. Now, why do you bother? Why memorize all those dumb lyrics?"

She was shocked. "Dumb lyrics! Songs are everything. They're how people express their emotions: love, pain, hope. They're people's dreams. I already told you, man, I'm gonna become the singing minstrel of California, traveling from town to town and singing all the songs so people never forget what's important. Like love and friendship. I'll be reminding them who they were, what they still can be. Like a photo album of their emotions."

Eric nodded. "So what you're doing is providing a history for people. A past they can tap into for strength. Like a well people can keep going back to for a cool drink."

"Yeah, that's a neat way of putting it. A cool drink."

"Well, all knowledge is from the same well. Knowing where flamingos get their pink is the same as

61

knowing what Kierkegaard thought about Existentialism."

She made a face. "I'll think about it."

"Good, because that's enough talk. Let's grab a bird and get the hell out of here."

"Don't you want to shop around first? Christ, this is like a supermarket. Maybe we could get some lamb."

"This isn't a supermarket, D.B. It's a jungle. We don't know who else is here or what animals may be loose."

"Loose?"

"Free of their cages or exhibits. The quakes could have drained the moats or crumbled the walls that enclosed many of the dangerous animals."

She touched her choke collar. "I hadn't thought about that. I'm so used to seeing them on display." She looked around nervously.

Eric handed her the crossbow. "You keep guard while I grab the flamingo. Then we go back up the wall and out. Ready?"

She nodded.

Eric ran silently across the courtyard. He saw the gift shops, the restaurants, the turnstiles. He tried to concentrate on the sleeping flamingos, but the memories started to come back, stuck in his throat like barbed hooks. Annie. Jenny. Tim. The four of them wandering through the zoo on the Saturday morning. Before coming, each had taken a specialty to study and share with the others. Annie had taken reptiles because she'd had a turtle as a child. Jenny had taken birds (she had told them all how the flamingos got their pink). Tim had insisted on primates. Eric had taken cats. They'd had so much fun impressing each other with what they'd learned. Annie even had notes, which she referred to secretly when the kids weren't looking, shoving her glasses on and reading from her notebook. Tim and Jenny started well, but after a while got their information mixed up. Finally, they all started to make up facts, each trying to top the other with a more absurd animal "fact." "The porcupine," Annie had lectured, imitating Eric's classroom stance, "once had the softest coat of fur of any other animal. Until it became known among the other animals as 'nature's toilet paper.' To protect itself from their abuse, it evolved the prickly quills we see today."

They had all thrown popcorn at her.

Eric forced the memory away, concentrating on the flamingo. One quick snap of its head and it would be dead. He could throw it over his shoulder, holding onto the long skinny legs, and be over the wall again in less than a minute. If everything went according to plan.

It didn't.

7

It chuffed like a steam locomotive. Huffing and grunting in the darkness, coming closer.

Eric stopped in mid-run to look around. He didn't see anything, yet he felt something coming at him. Its energy and power. Its dark intent. He turned back to D.B. "Give me the bow."

She started to hand it to him, but it was already too late.

It dropped out of an overhead tree, landed with a ground-shaking thud beside Eric, and knocked him to the ground with a flick of its huge arm.

Eric sprawled across the grass, sliding into the flock of flamingos. They ruffled their feathers, then stalked away on their stilted legs. Eric roused himself with some difficulty, shaking the fuzziness from his head. The blow that had hurled him to the ground had merely been a brush, but it had come from a 6-foot, 400-pound, silverback gorilla that stood in front of him now, baring its fanged teeth at him, rearing back on its legs to thump its chest at Eric.

D.B. lifted the crossbow and sighted down the arrow. "Should I shoot it?" she asked.

"Damn right," Eric said. "And don't miss."

"You pull that trigger," a woman's voice warned, "and I'll put a bullet through your head."

Eric and D.B. turned to face the woman. She was short, barely five feet. Her black hair was woven into one long braid, thick as rope, that hung past her waist. Her accent was British, but her face was strictly Oriental, smooth as a river stone. She looked jumpy, but in control. Eric had no doubt she would shoot. "Put the bloody bow down," she said, motioning at D.B. with her gun.

D.B. laid the bow on the ground.

The gorilla rocked side to side, leaning on its knuckles.

Eric started to stand up. He spoke calmly to the woman. "There's been some mistake—"

The woman jumped back as if Eric's movement were threatening. Suddenly she tucked the gun under her arm and said, "Spock!"

The gorilla looked over at her. She made a gesture with her hands: her right hand was an open claw which she closed as she brought it downward in a catching motion, ending with it bumping the back of her other hand.

The gorilla immediately lunged at Eric. Its thick hairy arms wrapped around Eric's body, pinning his arms to his chest. It huffed foul air in his face as it squeezed tighter and tighter. Eric struggled, writhed, kicked at its knees. No use. It sat down, rolled onto its back and continued to crush Eric. He felt his ribs bending, his vertebrae shifting under the enormous pressure. His face was buried in the ape's furry chest. It smelled like old carpet left out in the rain. Eric felt as small

65

and helpless as a Cabbage Patch doll.

Eric's legs went numb. He tasted oily metallic blood in his mouth. He could only manage to inhale a slight gasp of breath.

The gorilla kept squeezing.

Book Two:

THE ZOOKEEPERS

One trembles to think of that mysterious thing in the soul, which seems to acknowledge no human jurisdiction . . .

Herman Melville

8

Dirk Fallows tapped the pocket watch with the tip of his knife. He smiled. " 'Saint-seducing gold.' "

The man who had given him the watch nodded nervously. "Solid gold, Colonel."

Fallows laughed. " 'Saint-seducing gold.' That's a line from *Romeo and Juliet*. Are you familiar with the work?"

"Sure," the man shrugged. "Like *The West Side Story*, only no music."

"Close enough," Fallows said and continued examining the watch. He sat at a small folding card table on the northern outskirts of San Diego, the best central location for those who would come to sell gold.

The line of sellers stretched fifty yards long, wrapping around one of the supply tents. Each vendor carried an item of gold. Some had silver or precious stones. These were not worth as much, but word was out that Fallows would accept them. The campsite was run like a military operation, with Fallows' armed men stationed around the supply tent.

Fallows himself sat alone at the table, a box to the

left with the valuables he'd purchased: silverware, jewelry, gold picture frames. He had no gun on the table. It was as if he couldn't comprehend someone trying to defy him.

Gordon Hamilton, the man with the pocket watch, waited while Fallows turned the watch over and over in his hand. For twenty-three of his forty-five years Gordon had been a custodian at Crescent Hills High School, a school whose only claim to fame was a championship chess team, which made them the laughing stock of the rest of the schools. Gordon had swept the gym a lot of times (4,140 times unofficially), listening to the same old pep talks from coach after coach, to team after team. The results were always the same. Basketball, last place. Football, third from last place. Volleyball, last place.

The quakes had torn Crescent Hills High School in half, ripping the gymnasium right along the half-court line. It had happened in the middle of cheerleading practice, which was no great loss since their cheerleaders were uglier than their football team.

Gordon's watch had been a gift from the school district for twenty years of service. Solid 24-k gold; the principal had said at the luncheon (dinners were reserved for teachers and administrators), then pretended to bite on it like an old prospector. Everyone had laughed, including Gordon.

Dirk Fallows was staring at him and Gordon swallowed nervously. The saliva felt like a lump of cement scraping down his throat. Fallows' stare reminded Gordon of the way some lizards look at you, their eyes kind of dead but hungry, their leathery mouths upturned, almost a smile, like they know they're going to eat you and there's not a goddamn thing you can do about it.

Gordon felt sweat dripping down his forehead but he didn't wipe it away. He didn't want to appear as nervous as he was. Others in the line were jostling impatiently, anxious to trade whatever trinket they had for some canned corned beef hash, Campbells soup, packs of cigarettes.

"Shut up back there," Fallows said. The line immediately settled down. Fallows looked up from the watch and stared at Gordon. There was that lizard grin, Gordon thought. That and the long V-shaped face, all bone and angles, made him look like a face stamped on some ancient Roman coin. The short, bristly white hair, premature for a guy in his mid-forties, looked like a shiny helmet. A gladiator, Gordon decided, that's what he looks like. A guy who can't wait to go back into the arena again.

Gordon was avoiding Fallows' stare when he saw someone approach. A tall lanky kid in his late teens, but no, as the kid got closer he could see the boy was only about fifteen or sixteen. Gordon had been around kids this age for more than twenty years and was pretty good at guessing ages. Lots of kids these days were tall for their ages. This one was just a couple inches short of Gordon's own six-foot two inches. But this kid was not just tall, he was remarkably muscled. His chest stretched the green t-shirt. The waist was narrow, but flared over hard sinewy thighs. The arms were lumpy and veined.

But it was the face that shocked Gordon. It was a child's face all right, but the expression wasn't a child's. It was blank, withdrawn. Yet beneath the controlled facial muscles, the eyes were dark and brooding. Gordon had seen eyes like that on the kids at school who had been expelled, arrested, sent to hospitals.

71

"Tim," Fallows said, handing him the watch as he approached. "What do you think?"

Tim silently examined the watch.

"Gold," Fallows said to Gordon. "A remarkable substance. One ounce can be beaten out to three hundred square feet. When it's that thin it would transmit a greenish light, like the eyes of some women I've known. About sixty percent of the mined gold in the world is in the hands of governments and central banks. Did you know that?"

Gordon shook his head. What was taking so long? He just wanted a few cans of food, maybe some of those canned spaghettis. The kid, Tim, was digging at the watch with his thumbnail.

Fallows continued. "Now most gold in jewelry has some silver in it, or paladium, or platinum. Alloys like that can be twelve, fourteen, sixteen, on up to twenty-four karats. Twelve is only fifty percent gold. Twenty-four is pure gold. I asked only for the pure stuff because I don't have the time or manpower to fuck around with junk. Right?"

Gordon and everyone else in line nodded.

Fallows smiled. "Good. As long as we understand each other." He looked up at Tim. "Well? What's the verdict?"

Tim set the watch on the table. "Twelve karats."

"Oops. You sure? This man tells me it's twenty-four."

Tim shrugged. "Twelve."

Fallows returned his gaze to Gordon. Gordon instinctively took a step back.

"It's gotta be more. They told me it was solid gold. A solid gold watch, they said, for twenty years of solid gold service. I swear."

Fallows chuckled. "Perhaps your service was only

72

gold-plated." He tossed the watch to Gordon. "Get out."

Gordon hesitated, looked pleadingly at Tim. Tim stared back with cold indifference. Like I'm a bug, Gordon thought, like a bug squashed on a windshield. Someone behind him nudged him out of the way, dumping a handful of rings and earrings on the table.

"Got 'em out of some Beverly Hills mansion," the man said. "They was locked in a safe, only the quakes had shook that safe clean outta the wall. Cracked open like an egg shell. These was inside."

Gordon wandered to the side of the line. A few looked at him with sympathy, but most with contempt. He wasn't sure which he loathed more, the sympathy or the contempt. They all knew now, knew that his gold watch for twenty years of service with the fucking school district had only been worth a cheap watch. Worse, they thought him so dumb they even lied to him about it. For the last three years of working there he'd carried the watch at school, having even bought a vest to keep it in, the gold (12 karat) chain dangling down. He'd worn it proudly, something to show for all the gum he'd scraped off desks, the cigarettes students had bummed from him in the restroom. The toilets he'd unclogged from girls flushing tampons.

"Tim?" Fallows said.

Tim bent over and pawed through the jewelry. He held a couple of rings up to the light, scratched the surface of the earrings. "These two rings are good. All the earrings are."

"Very good," Fallows said. "My assessment exactly." Fallows took the good ones and flung the bad ones into the bushes. The man's eyes followed them but he stifled an urge to go after them. Fallows brushed the jewelry into one hand and dumped it in the cardboard box at his side. "Go over to the supply tent and help yourself to six cans of anything."

"You got bourbon?" the man asked.

"One bottle's all you get."

"Hell, I'll take it." He jogged over to the tent where two armed men escorted him inside.

Gordon Hamilton sulked off, walking slow and shuffling his feet in the dirt. He kicked at a stone like a little boy. He felt like a little boy. A boy who'd been cheated and now humiliated. All my life, he thought, it's been like that. someone in charge making me do stuff. All my life. What a phrase. When you started saying that, your life was about over. He felt the anger welling in him, a dark surge of heat rushing up his stomach and spreading over his chest. He was shaking. He thought about the luncheon, about the watch, about Fallows, about the kid, Tim. The months of scratching for survival, the whole time keeping that watch no matter what because it was a symbol, a symbol of what he'd meant before. That what he'd done had had some value, that he'd counted. Twelve fucking karats! His anger and hatred boiled up through his head. Even his eyeballs felt dry. His head ached.

He reached inside his jacket for his gun.

Even as he did, he knew he was being foolish.

Worse, suicidal.

But he couldn't stop himself.

It was like breathing.

He removed the gun with its two .22 bullets in it. He turned.

As he raised the gun and cocked the hammer, he saw Fallows reach for his own gun. Gordon smiled knowing it would be too late. He was already squeezing the trigger. Fallows hand was barely on the grip. His men were too startled to react. They fumbled with their fancy rifles.

Gordon fired. The sound of the explosion was like a release. All his hatred and anger whoosed out of his body behind the bullet.

But he hadn't counted on the kid. Tim.

Tim's expression never changed as he moved, shouldering Fallows out of the way like a football tackle bringing down the quarterback. Fallows tumbled to the ground with Tim on top of him. Gordon's bullet whizzed by the table and dug itself into the box of gold trinkets. Gordon realized he'd missed, swung the gun around at Fallows.

By now Fallows had his gun out of the holster. He fired three times, each bullet shredding another section of Gordon Hamilton's chest. Gordon looked down at the leaking holes in his body and smiled. At least he missed the watch. Then he died.

Fallows was on his feet and kneeling next to Gordon's body, his gun pressed to the dead man's head as he felt for a pulse. "Son of a bitch is dead," Fallows said firing a bullet into Gordon's head. "One to grow on, asshole."

Fallows got up and looked at the half dozen of his men who were now gathered around the scene, their guns covering the crowd. "Never mind them," he shouted at them. "Where were you ten seconds ago, when this maniac was trying to kill me?" He walked over to Tim who was brushing dirt from his pants. "Hadn't been for the kid here I'd be dead."

Fallows' men didn't say anything. It wouldn't do any good to apologize. Fallows did not accept excuses. At any minute he might open fire on them as an example to others. Even armed as they were with six of them against him, none thought their chances of survival against an alerted Fallows was even a remote possibility. They'd all seen him work before.

They waited.

Fallows laughed, threw his arm around Tim's shoulder. "You're really learning, Tim. Those are fast reflexes. Faster than me or Eric."

At the mention of his father's name, Tim shrugged off Fallows' arm and walked off toward the woods. He knew Fallows was watching him, but that he wouldn't follow. Why bother? There was nowhere to go. Tim had tried many times to escape, but each time they'd caught him and brought him back to hours of slow torture by Fallows. The cuts, the burns, the starvation. Eventually Tim stopped trying. Then his food rations were increased. Fallows had stepped up the lessons, expanding them to include all phases of combat and survival. His muscles had grown along with his height. Tim had to admit, he liked his new body, as manly as any of Fallows' soldiers. If he were still back at school he could be on any junior varsity team he wanted: basketball, volleyball, wrestling.

Tim sat on an uprooted tree trunk. He could name all the plants within sight, knew how to use them to eat, drink, kill. Much of that knowledge Eric had already taught him, or Big Bill Tenderwolf had on their visits, but before it had just been useless information. Now it all made sense. Knowledge was power; power was survival. Fallows had taught him that.

In the evenings they played chess together, just as Tim used to do with his father. Fallows favored the Caro-Kann Defense or Sicilian Attack. Eric's game had been more patient, flexible. In a match between his father and Fallows he wasn't sure who would win, any more than he knew who would win this battle between them now. Any more than he knew why he had saved Fallows' life.

Saved his life. The man who had killed his mother and sister. Who had tortured him. Who was trying to kill his father.

Tim had saved *him*.

Saved Fallows!

Tim felt the tears flood his eyes. He blinked and sent them cascading down his cheeks. Nothing made sense. Where was his father? It had been months since that last rescue attempt. Tim rubbed his leg where Fallows had shot him. The scar was still there, like a white crater pasted on the back of his thigh. Still, it was Fallows who kept him alive now, who taught him things. Eric had had Big Bill Tenderwolf as a teacher; Tim had Fallows. It was Fallows who made sure everyone else treated Tim with respect. Even the other soldiers were a little afraid of Tim because of Fallows. And every village or settlement they marched through, people cowered, gave them anything they wanted. Those who fought always lost. Fallows had no mercy. They had a reputation now. He could see the panic and fear in people's eyes when they saw Fallows' men. Tim liked that feeling of power. After all these months of helplessness, it felt good to have some control.

What about his father? What about Eric Ravensmith?

"Tim," Fallows said.

Tim turned. He hadn't heard Fallows walk up. No one ever did.

"Thinking?"

Tim nodded.

"A rare exercise around here."

Tim looked at Fallows. It was something Eric might have said. Did Fallows know that? Was this part of the chess match?

Fallows sat down on the log next to him. "I appreciate what you did back there. You've become a first-rate soldier."

"I didn't stop to think."

Fallows ignored the implication. "That's the mark of a good soldier. Reaction. Muscle memory. The body moving before the mind slows it down."

Tim shrugged. "It's done."

"Yes, it's done. Now what?"

"What do you mean?"

"Do you keep fighting me, or do you join me? Accept that it's better to rule in hell than serve in heaven."

"John Milton said that. My dad taught me."

"What would he answer to that?"

Tim thought a moment. "Probably that it's better to rule in heaven."

Fallows laughed. "Yes, that's exactly what he would say." Then Fallows' face went grim. "But he was always overambitious. In trying to doublecross me, in trying to protect his family, in trying to get you back." Fallows stood up. "My ambitions are more modest. But they come true."

Tim didn't say anything. There was truth to what Fallows said. But it felt like a trap, a possible checkmate in three moves.

"We're going back into San Diego again. We have enough gold for now. I think maybe it's time to get you a woman. Interested?"

Tim turned away. How many nights had he listened

78

while the others had taken women (and sometimes boys) in their tents. Sometimes he heard the moans of pleasure, sometimes the shrieks of pain and terror, depending on the mood of the men and how rough they were. At first they had kept Tim tied up, now they let him roam about, though there was always one or two men keeping him in sight. Tim had to admit, there were times when he felt an urge, a need to be next to a girl.

"You can decide later," Fallows said. "Meantime, you'll need this." He took his Walther out of his holster and tossed it to Tim. Tim caught it by the grip. The last time Fallows had given him a gun, Tim had fired at Fallows. But the gun had been empty, a trick. Now Tim just held it. "It's loaded," Fallows assured him. "If you shot me now, there wouldn't be anything I could do about it."

Tim looked at the gun. The clip was in. But were there any bullets in the clip? Perhaps Fallows had a sniper in the brush with his sights trained on Tim's back.

"Go ahead, Tim. Check the clip."

Tim released the clip. It was full. He slapped it back into the grip. The firing pin could be busted, he thought.

Fallows laughed, as if he could read Tim's mind. "Shoot it at a tree. It works."

But Tim knew it would fire. He knew the gun was perfect, he could tell from the look in Fallows' eyes. He could shoot him right now, kill him. Then why didn't he?

Checkmate.

"It's yours now, Tim," Fallows said, turning his back and walking toward the camp.

Tim watched him go. He thought about shooting,

but the gun seemed so damn heavy, impossible to lift. Then Fallows was gone.

Tim stuffed the gun in his waistband and followed Fallows back to camp.

9

Eric kicked the wire cage. It flexed but did not break. Next door they could hear the frantic chatter of monkeys hooting and scampering around their own cage. Eric kicked the wire mesh again and the monkeys' voices rose excitedly.

"Think they're laughing at us?" D.B. asked, sitting in the corner.

"Why not?" Eric said. "I am."

He continued to explore the small room. It was about the size of a walk-in closet. The other three walls of their prison were beige cement, too solid to break through. He tested the strength of the wire mesh again, then inspected the small feeding door at the back of the cage. The whole building was a series of such rooms, each facing out so the spectators could walk all the way around the building viewing the different types of monkeys.

"What now, bwanna?" D.B. asked.

Eric was on hands and knees, rapping on the feeding door, looking for weaknesses. "Maybe you could lead us all in a rousing chorus of 'We Shall Overcome.'"

"I'd like to overcome this smell. Christ, what do these apes do?"

"Guess."

She made a face. "Yuck. I thought they were supposed to be so clean, you know, the way you always see them picking fleas outta each other's fur."

Frustrated, Eric stood up and kicked at the feeding door, which brought nothing more than another enthusiastic clamor from their neighbors and a searing jolt of pain along Eric's tender ribs. He sighed and sat down next to D.B. "They're not picking fleas, they're grooming. Big difference."

"Grooming, huh? Like one of them is a hairdresser or something? They all call him Mr. Chimp?"

Eric laughed. "Something like that. It's partially hygiene, but mostly socializing. Sometimes they do it just to soothe each other, like massages. Sometimes it's a matter of social status. Depending on your rank in the group, you mostly either give or get. Females have it worse. They groom the male for about ten minutes, he gives them back an obligatory 30 seconds, then they give him another ten minutes."

"The usual male bullshit," she teased.

"Just remember that it's a woman who's got us locked up in here."

D.B. reached over and gently placed her hand on Eric's sore ribs. "How they holding up? You took some heavy tenderizing from that ape."

"At least I showed him who was higher on the evolutionary scale."

"Yeah," she laughed. "It was clever the way you let him tire himself out crushing you."

Eric took a deep breath, felt the sharp sting as his lungs expanded against his battered ribcage. He could still feel those hard bristly arms coiled around his body. He was sure that if he lifted his shirt he would discover the perfect imprints of thick primate muscles on his bruised skin, every sinew perfectly embedded as if in wet sand.

82

"When's feeding time around here?" D.B. asked. "I'm hungry."

"You think she'll waste precious food on us?"

"Tarzana? Sure, she'll feed us. Why starve us to death? She could've shot us last night, or let her ape do the mashed potato on our heads."

Eric looked at her and smiled. "Tarzana?"

"That's what I call her. Like Queen of the Apes. Maybe she was with a circus or something. An animal trainer."

"Not likely. She used American Sign Language with the ape. That takes years of working with the same animal. Very specialized. She was probably with the zoo. Research maybe."

D.B. had already lost interest in that topic. She fidgeted with her choke collar. "You think she's a looker?"

Eric shrugged. "A little hairy, maybe, but sure."

"I mean Tarzana. I'm no smart-ass history prof, but even I could tell that ape was a male." She nudged Eric. "C'mon. Answer me."

Eric could see she was serious. Sometimes it was hard to remember that even here in the violent world under the Halo, kids still had the same growing pains as those outside. "Yes. She is attractive."

D.B. nodded wisely. "Guys always go for those Oriental types."

"I'm not going for anything, except your throat if you don't knock it off. Let's concentrate on getting out of here."

"Sure. Got any ideas?" She smiled at him. "We could use my head for a battering ram."

Eric reached over and mussed her hair. "What wall would stand a chance?" He stood up, pressed his face against the wire, looked both ways. "I don't see her anywhere. Let's try kicking on that feeding door together."

They lay on their backs next to each other, their knees tucked up to their chins.

Eric counted. "One, two, *three* . . ." On three, they both stomped their feet straight ahead, whacking the door with all four feet. But to no effect. The door remained locked.

They tried again. And again.

Nothing.

D.B. rolled away, hugging her sore feet. "I'll never polka again."

Eric kicked the door a few more times by himself. He knew it was no use, but he had to try something. The monkeys next door were screeching and wailing like irate neighbors in an apartment building.

"Uh oh," D.B. said. "Guess who's coming to dinner."

Eric turned, saw the huge silverback ape who'd bounced him around last night. The ape ambled up and pressed his leathery face against the cage. He peered in, tilting his head quizzically.

Eric and D.B. slowly climbed to their feet, the ape watching them with obvious curiosity. His head was large, the huge flared nostrils looking like twin volcano craters. The corneas of his eyes were tinted red. His head and body were covered with shaggy black fur, except for a saddle of silver fur spanning his back.

The monkeys in the adjoining cages were practically hysterical now, screaming and thumping. The big silverback hopped backward a few steps, glared at the monkeys on both sides. They fell silent. The gorilla waddled back to D.B. and Eric's cage.

D.B. looked him over. "Once you get used to the smell, he's kinda cute."

Eric didn't respond. He was staring at the ape,

thinking.

D.B. recognized his stance. The grim expression, the fixed eyes. He was changing even as she watched him. Not like those Lon Chaney movies where he turns into a wolfman with hair sprouting out of his forehead. The change in Eric was more subtle, yet just as dramatic. He was changing from the amiable professor, the caring companion, the big brother; changing into something primal, almost a state of pure energy. It was how she imagined him in Vietnam when he was with that elite group of government assassins, Night Shift.

His face tightened into a cold, hard visage, as stony as a primitive Mayan mask. The lips stretched thin and sharp. The white scar on his cheek pulsed like a slow crack working its way across a frozen glacier.

D.B. stepped back. Away from both of them. When he was like this his power was frightening. His concentration was so acute that his personality seemed to be snuffed out under the brighter hotter fire of his will. Gone was the sense of humor, the compassion. What was left was deadly efficiency.

The ape seemed to sense the change in Eric too. He rocked side to side, standing hunched, leaning on his knuckles. He curled his rubbery lips up, baring his chunky teeth at Eric.

Eric took a step toward the ape. He made some hand movements D.B. didn't understand: he opened his right hand with his palm facing left, then dragged the tip of his thumb down his jawline, flicking the hand down to chest level. He repeated this three times.

The ape stared at Eric. He no longer bared his teeth. Instead he seemed a little calmer. He sat down in front of the cage.

"It's working," D.B. said, relieved.

Eric didn't answer her. He started making a different hand movement: he opened his left hand, palm down; he stuck the index finger of his right hand straight out, pressed it under the flat left hand, and shoved it forward in a stabbing motion.

The ape leaped to his feet and slammed his fists into the cage. He threw his head back, pursed his lips, and started hooting. The monkeys in the other cages made frightened skittering noises. The giant black gorilla ran over to a nearby tree, yanked a few leaves off and pretended to eat. He threw the leaves away, grabbed a branch, tore it from the tree, and threw it against the cage. It bounced off the wire.

Eric continued to make the same hand movements. This only enraged the ape more. He beat his chest a few times. The sound was surprisingly loud, echoing like rolling thunder. He began stomping his feet and beating his chest in unison. He ran sideways back and forth, finally picking up a yellow trash can with "Pitch in!" stenciled on the side and hurling it at the cage.

D.B. ducked, even though the trash can bounced harmlessly off the wire mesh. "This isn't working, Doc," she said, hugging the wall. "Go back to the first signal. He liked that."

But Eric's concentration was impenetrable. He took another step closer to the ape and started combining the two hand signals in sharp, emphatic gestures. First one, then the other. Over and over. This enraged the ape even more. He ran around uprooting plants, tossing leaves and branches into the air like a madman.

Then he came back to the cage.

He was huffing now, air panting from his mouth in angry puffs. He glared at Eric. Suddenly he raised his right hand high over his head and slapped it palm down on the ground with a resounding thump. He sat back and waited. Obviously it was Eric's move now.

Eric walked up to the wire mesh that separated the two of them. They were less than a foot apart now, their eyes locked in communication that bridges all species. Eric gestured with the same two hand signs again, repeating the combination over and over.

The ape jumped up, roared, and charged the wire.

"Jesus Christ!" D.B. screamed, flattening herself against the rear wall.

Even Eric backed up now, though not out of fear. Each step was slow and deliberate. She thought he was almost smiling.

The gorilla clawed at the wire, poking thick black fingers through, trying to rip the wire loose. He butted his head into the wire, yanked on it, tried to climb it, even attempted to chew it.

Then the wire started to rip.

"He's getting in!" D.B. hollered.

Eric nodded calmly. "That's the plan."

"What fucking plan? He gets in, eats us, and we escape in his stomach?"

Eric repeated the hand signals and the ape redoubled his efforts to get at them.

"Stop that," D.B. said. "He gets the point."

Eric looked over at her as if he didn't understand her panic. "Trust me," he said.

"Forget it, mister. I've seen that movie before. No survivors."

The wire had stretched and buckled and the 400-pound ape was jerking on it with all his might. Within seconds he would be inside their cage.

"One of us has to occupy him," Eric said, "while the other gets out."

"Define occupy." D.B. looked at Eric. His expression was blank as if he hadn't yet decided which of them would do the occupying and which the escaping. It didn't matter. The ape had torn a large enough hole in the wire that, with some effort, he could squeeze through. All decisions would now be his.

But while the gorilla was twisted sideways, trying to bully his lumpy body through the wire, Eric charged straight for him. He spun around, whipping his right foot in a slashing arc that caught the ape on the jaw and knocked him sideways. A little. The ape seemed more surprised than hurt. Eric charged again, snapping two sidekicks into the stunned animals' head. Blood trickled from the ape's mouth.

"Ready?" Eric asked D.B.

"For what?"

"As soon as he pops in here, you run out and jump the wall."

"What about you?"

He smiled. "I'll be right behind you."

The silverback was almost inside now. His right leg was caught, the thick matted fur snagged on the torn wire. He roared angrily, yanking on his leg, and it scraped through the jagged wire leaving tufts of black fur capping the metal ends.

He was inside.

The room had been small before, now it was suffocating. Like the graves in the cemetery they'd run away from. D.B. backed into the side wall and waited for Eric's lead. Her legs wobbled so much she wasn't sure she'd be able to move when the time came.

Eric faced the ape, not giving an inch. He spoke calmly to D.B. as if he were discussing the history of a plant. His calmness helped her find some strength. "Just slip around him when it's clear and jump through the wire."

D.B. nodded. "Sure, simple enough. Squeeze by a four hundred pound gorilla without him noticing." Slowly she inched along the wall, her back scraping the cement.

Eric balled his fingers into fists. He had no intention of sacrificing himself to this hairy monster. Tim was still out there somewhere. So was Fallows.

Now that he was inside, the ape seemed a little cautious. Blood still dripped from his lip as he stalked Eric, leaning on one set of knuckles while lifting his free hand like a club. The heavy arm swooshed at Eric just as he dodged away, but the ape was faster than Eric thought. He whipped his arm back immediately and caught Eric on the shoulder, knocking him into the wall. Eric rose shakily.

"I'm going to charge him," he told D.B. "That's when you go. Ready?"

D.B. nodded.

"Now!" Eric lunged at the ape, dropping to the ground and sweeping his leg behind it, whacking the backs of the ape's knees. It was an old trick Big Bill Tenderwolf had taught him. "Old Hopi fighting technique," he'd explained. Eric had said, "I saw Bruce Lee do it in *Enter the Dragon*." To which Big Bill had shrugged and said, "Bruce Lee is half Hopi. I thought everyone knew."

The ape stumbled to his knees and D.B. bolted for the wire. Her skinny body slipped through easily and she darted for the wall.

Eric hesitated. He could easily take advantage of the moment and kill the ape with a crushing blow to the windpipe, or even blind it with a thumb-gouge to the eyes. It would be so simple, take only a second. Size and strength didn't matter in such matters, only anatomy. Death was mathematical. Cut off the air, it dies. No more threat.

Last night the ape had crushed him, but not out of malice. It had followed the Oriental woman's command to immobilize him. And it had done so playfully, as if it were all a delicious game. Now, sprawled on the floor, it looked angry, confused, frustrated. Like Eric.

Leaving the ape, Eric ran for the opening in the wire. It was harder going out than coming in because the ape's body had bent the wires inward, the jagged edges lined up like thorns. Eric pried them apart and stuck one leg through, slowly easing his body after.

Suddenly a heavy thump hit his back and he was propelled through the wire slot, the metal raking skin and shredding clothes. He slid chest-down along the pavement, lifting his head enough to avoid scraping off the skin. When he stopped sliding, he flipped over in time to see the ape jump out of the cage and run toward him. Eric cursed his own weakness in not killing it.

Even Eric's speed and agility were no match for the ape's anger. In two bounds it was on Eric, flashing teeth and swinging both arms. The first double blow just grazed Eric's back as he was trying to roll out of the way, but the force was enough to drop him flat. Eric lashed out with a desperate punch to the ape's nose, but there wasn't much of a nose to damage. The surprise of the blow made the ape pause, but that was all. Then he slammed a fist down on Eric's thigh and the leg went numb.

"Stop it!" D.B. cried.

Eric saw her standing behind the ape now. She was swinging the branch he'd earlier torn from the tree. The branch thudded into the ape's silver back and he looked around, annoyed. She swung again.

While the ape was distracted, Eric scooted out of

his reach. D.B. whacked him again with the branch. A cloud of dust puffed from his fur with each blow, as if she were beating a rug. The ape grabbed for her. She poked the branch at him and he snatched it from her, jumping up and down with it while she backed away.

"Run for the wall!" Eric told her.

She did.

The ape took a couple of steps in her direction but Eric tossed the yellow trash can at him. It bounced off the ape's head. He turned back to Eric, rubbing the back of his head.

D.B. was almost to the wall.

The ape was scowling at Eric, coming toward him. Eric eyed his throat. One clear shot, he thought, that's all I need.

"Spock!" the woman's voice called.

The ape looked up. The Oriental woman was running toward them. She drew her gun from her holster and pointed it at D.B. "Get away from that wall or I'll shoot."

D.B. was just at the base of the wall. She stopped, held up her hands.

Tucking the gun under her arm a moment, the woman faced the ape, making sure he was looking at her, even at twenty yards away. She made a chopping motion with her right hand into the palm of her left. "Stop," she said slowly, repeating the motion. "Stop."

The ape stood still.

She gripped the gun again and approached cautiously. She waved D.B. over, waiting until they stood next to each other with their hands up before walking closer. When she saw the blood on the ape's lips, she pointed the gun at Eric's face. "You bastard, you've hurt him."

"He's a real brute sometimes," D.B. said.

"You think it's funny?" the woman said, flipping a curtain of long black hair over her shoulder. "I should shoot you both right now."

"We only wanted out of here," Eric said.

"Then why did you come in in the first place?"

"Food," D.B. said.

The woman's dark eyes glared at D.B. "This is not a supermarket. These are living creatures, most very rare." Her British accent tattered a little with her anger, her Chinese origins showing through.

"Look," Eric said. "We were hungry. We made a mistake. You let us go and we'll be on our way, no harm done."

"The harm's already been done." She motioned with the gun. "Now I'll have to find another cage for you two. How did you manage to tear that one open?"

"We didn't," D.B. said. "He did."

"Spock?" she said. "Impossible. He would never attack you."

"He doesn't take a joke well," Eric said.

"Joke? What joke?"

Eric repeated the signs he'd made that had enraged the ape.

"Woman," she said, reading the first. Then the second, "Dead. Killed." She jabbed the gun against Eric's chest. "You told him I was dead!"

"Wow," D.B. said. "No wonder he was so pissed."

"We couldn't break out," Eric said, "so I needed him to break in."

The woman spat out a long stream of Chinese, to which Eric answered in Chinese.

"Shit," D.B. said. "I shoulda known."

The woman gazed at Eric thoughtfully. "You learn your Chinese in Vietnam?"

"Thereabouts."

"You have a Vietnamese inflection."

"I'll work on it. You learn your English in Oxford?"

"Cambridge."

D.B. sighed disgustedly. "Ain't this sweet. A class reunion for eggheads."

The woman ignored D.B. "So, you speak Chinese. And you know Ameslan."

"Ameslan?" D.B. asked.

"American Sign Language," Eric said. Then to the woman, "I know enough Chinese to keep the peanut shrimp from being too spicy The Ameslan is something I picked up to communicate with my deaf students."

"How altruistic," she said, a disbelieving edge to her voice.

"The school paid me extra for it if that'll make you feel better." It was a lie of course. Yes, he knew Ameslan, but he'd learned it in the Night Shift from Dirk Fallows. A silent way to communicate in the jungle while stalking your prey. Big Bill Tenderwolf had taught him some Hopi sign language, but very few knew it anymore except historians. Even Big Bill used to get it mixed up, signing, "Let's go get a drink of turtle."

D.B. tugged her choke collar. "Listen, let's wrap this up, okay? Our names are—"

"No!" the woman said. "I don't want to know names."

"Well, shit, even your ape's got a name. Spock."

At the name, the ape looked at D.B.

"See? You a trekkie?"

"What she means, D.B., is she doesn't want us to be personal, with names and such, in case she has to kill us. Right?"

"You came to kill my animals. I need make no

excuses." She held her five feet stiff and defiant, like the gun. "You aren't the first to come here. Only one ever managed to kill and he in turn was killed by Spock."

"And the others?" Eric asked, suddenly interested.
"Secure."

He took a step toward her. "Where?"

She cocked the gun and aimed it at his face. "Stay there. I'll shoot."

He kept coming.

She pulled the trigger.

10

The hammer clicked on an empty chamber.

"Bang," Eric said. He plucked the gun from her hand.

Spock, the gorilla, lumbered forward with a menacing expression.

"This may be empty," Eric said, brandishing the gun, "but a pistol whipping can really mess up his face."

The woman stared at Eric a moment. She signed to the ape and he sat down. She shook her head at Eric. "You don't bluff easily."

"Oh, I don't know. You got away with it last night. Though I should have suspected when you risked your ape rather than just shoot us."

The woman shrugged. "I ran out of bullets months ago. Now I carry it for show. It usually works."

"Where's my bow?"

She pointed. "Back in the garden where I was weeding. I heard Spock's chest-thumping and hurried over without it."

D.B. shaded her eyes and looked in the direction the woman was pointing. "Where is this garden of yours?"

"The other side of the zoo, near Highway 163."

"That's a long way to hear."

"Not really," Eric said. "That sound can carry for a mile."

"One and a third miles," the woman corrected.

D.B. laughed. "How about that? Someone smarter than Doc Rock!"

The woman looked puzzled. "Doc Rock?"

"Nickname," Eric said. "That's D.B. I'm Eric Ravensmith."

"You ever hear of The Warlord?" D.B. asked her. She shook her head.

"Christ, lady, where you been? If there was a *People* magazine around here, this guy would be on the cover. I call him Doc Rock, though, because, well, look at him. Doesn't he remind you of rock-'n'-roll music? All that wild energy and ragged edges."

The woman looked at the two of them as if they were lunatics. "You said you wanted to go. So go."

"First, let's see those other intruders you talked about."

D.B. tugged at his arm. "First, let's eat."

"Later."

"Okay, but if I don't eat soon I'm gonna have to start talking with my fingers like Spock here." She reached out and tickled the ape. He chuckled and rolled over on his back, grasping his feet.

The woman studied Eric and D.B.

D.B. continued to tickle Spock. "I'm gonna keep this up till you show me your stash of bananas." Spock rolled playfully from side to side.

"Okay," the woman said. "I'll take you to them. I can't stop you anyway."

"What's your name?" Eric said.

"That's not important."

He handed her the gun. "I'll trade you. This for your name."

She looked surprised but took the gun. "A gun is

very valuable, even an empty one."

Eric shrugged.

"Wendy," the woman sighed. "Dr. Wendy Chen."

"Now, Dr. Chen," Eric said. "Let's see your other prisoners."

Dr. Chen led the way. "Follow me very carefully," she warned. "The quakes allowed a lot of animals to escape from their display areas. During the past year Spock and I have recaptured most of them and returned them to their repaired homes. However, a few animals have eluded us."

"Like what?" D.B. asked.

"A few koalas."

"You mean those Australian teddy bears?"

Dr. Chen shook her head. "They aren't bears, they're marsupials."

"They have pouches," Eric explained.

"Oh." D.B. smiled. "They're so cute."

"They also have long sharp claws," Dr. Chen said, marching ahead.

"What else is on the loose," Eric asked.

"A couple of orangutans. A Komodo monitor—"

"Commode monitor?" D.B. laughed. "Sounds like someone watching you on the toilet." She laughed again and Spock made a whooping sound too.

Eric grinned. "Finally someone who can imitate your laugh."

Spock made a sign with his hands, repeating it over and over.

"What's he saying?" D.B. asked.

Dr. Chen looked over her shoulder. "He wants you to tickle him again."

"Okay," D.B. said. She worked her fingers into the fur under Spock's arms. He whooped again, rolled onto his back. "You're not afraid of no commode watcher, are you Spocky?"

Dr. Chen spun around with an exasperated sigh. "A Komodo monitor is also known as a Komodo dragon. It's the largest living lizard in the world, nearly ten feet long. It has sharp, serrated teeth and formidable claws. In the wild they've been known to bring down one thousand-pound water buffalos."

"Oh."

"Now, can we get on with it? I don't want you two here any longer than necessary. It has taken me almost a year to rebuild the walls and capture many of the animals. I don't want outsiders spoiling everything."

They walked the entire length of the zoo, skirting the bird aviary that had not been damaged by the quakes. They passed the Ape Grotto where three pygmy chimpanzees were swinging on ropes and climbing the wood platform while two others slept in the sun. One of the grottos had a lone ape in it. Spock paused in front of it to look at the other ape.

"How come that one's not out here running around?" D.B. asked.

"That's Madonna."

"Like the singer?"

Dr. Chen gave her a sharp look. "Like the mother of Christ."

D.B. winked at Eric. "Oh yeah, The Mothers of Christ. I got one of their albums."

Dr. Chen ignored her and kept walking. When they arrived at Dr. Chen's garden, she began shouting furiously. "Oh no! Not again!" She ran down the rows of tomatoes, potatoes, strawberries, zucchini, cucumbers, and several other varieties of food. The garden was huge, at least half an acre. She'd constructed a fence around the entire garden, only one

98

section had been trampled down and the strawberries had been eaten, the careful rows stomped flat.

Dr. Chen spun around looking in the distance, her long black hair swinging around behind her like a pirate flag. "I know you're out there, Candy. You too, Red." She looked down at the busted fence. "Damn! That's the second time this week."

"Orangutans?"

She nodded. "Male and female." She looked up suddenly at Eric. "How'd you know?"

"I saw them." He pointed. "They were hiding in that brush."

Dr. Chen squinted, following Eric's extended finger. "That's pretty good vision. Learn that in the jungle?" Her tone was sharp.

"Learned it in the movies. As a kid I liked sitting in the balcony so I could drop popcorn on the people below. Only problem was we had a real small screen, hard to see from up there."

She turned away, fussed with the broken fence. "I'll have to fix this first. I don't want them coming back for dessert."

"What's the big deal?" D.B. said. "Why don't you send Spock here to catch them? You can do it, can't you Spocky?" She poked him in the ribs and he chuckled.

Dr. Chen's voice was tight. "An orangutan is about four feet tall and weighs one hundred-eighty pounds. Its arms are longer and stronger than its legs. They can crush a coconut in one hand."

"Boy, make a statement around here and you get a history. I'm a singer, okay, not a zoologist."

"Your weapon is over there," Dr. Chen pointed. "I'll take you to the prisoners as soon as I've mended this fence."

Eric gestured to D.B. who made a sour face but

finally went off after the crossbow and quiver of bolts. That left Eric alone with the woman.

"Let me help," he said, reaching for a strand of snapped wire.

She pushed him out of the way. "No. I can do it. I've managed for almost a year without any help."

"That doesn't mean help wouldn't be welcome."

"Not from you."

Eric stood next to her now, looking down at her small frame. She worked quickly and expertly with the wire, her nimble fingers twisting and tying the broken strands. Lean muscles flexed in her arms and legs. He could smell her sweat, rich and musky. "A brother or husband?" he asked.

She paused but didn't look up from her work. "Father."

"Where?"

"Saigon. He was with the *hat boi*."

"The Vietnamese opera."

"Of Chinese origin," she said emphatically. "My father was Chinese, not an easy thing to be in Vietnam. Hatred of Chinese domination over them is as strong and fierce as many of your Southerners over the Civil War. Still, he was a gifted singer." She looked up now, dark eyes moist as if covered with melting ice. "Someone slipped into our apartment one night and slit his throat. The job was so expert that my mother who slept beside him was never even disturbed from her sleep. Only the sticky blood drying on her fingers finally woke her." She stared accusingly at Eric. "A note was left condemning him as a spy. My father sang opera. He was not a spy."

Eric replied softly, "It wasn't me. I didn't kill your father."

"No, but someone like you. I can see the way you move, the way you handle yourself. You were not

100

just a foot soldier, a grunt. No, it was someone very much like you who stole into our home that night."

Eric stood motionless. She was right. It was someone like him. Not him, of course. Eric remembered each mission clearly. But the Night Shift had killed suspected spies before. Slit throats in bed, shot heads at dinner, bombed cars and even bicycles.

"My mother took us back to China afterward, hidden among a cargo of dead fish at the bottom of a boat. There we lived since I was thirteen."

"Until Cambridge University."

"Yes. That is when I left. I have not been back since."

Eric reached over and began helping her dig the fence post deeper into the ground. It took only a few minutes to fix the fence. By then D.B. and Spock returned with Eric's crossbow and bolts.

"It won't hold them, you know," Eric said.

Dr. Chen nodded. "I know. Not if they really want to get in. But they're pretty domesticated for orang-utans. They know the fence is more a statement than a real barrier. They'll keep away for a while anyway."

"Maybe you just oughta feed them more," D.B. said.

Dr. Chen laughed for the first time since they'd been there. Her mouth opened revealing straight white teeth. Her eyes crinkled until they almost disappeared. "Orangs can never eat enough. That's all they do. In the wild they spend almost every waking hour looking for food and grow to be an average of one hundred-sixty pounds. In a zoo, they can bloat up to three hundred-fifty pounds if not watched.

D.B. patted her own stomach. "I know how they feel. I used to pack away a few Twinkies after school myself." She poked Spock's massive stomach. "Been chowing down a little yourself, eh Spocky?"

Spock pointed his two index fingers toward each other and moved them up toward his neck.

"What's he saying?" D.B. asked.

"He likes your necklace," Dr. Chen said. "He wants it."

"How do you say, 'Forget it, pal'?"

Dr. Chen extended the index and middle fingers of her right hand, tapped them twice against her thumb, like an alligator snapping. D.B. mimicked the movement. Spock lowered his head into a sulk.

"This is great!" D.B. laughed. "You gotta teach me more."

Dr. Chen smiled. Eric was pleased to see it was friendly smile, her fear and hatred momentarily subdued by D.B.'s enthusiasm. The way to any teacher's heart is a curious student, even a teacher of apes.

"Spock knows about four hundred signs."

"Great, I'll teach him song lyrics. How about this one Spock: 'Gorillas Just Wanna Have Fun'?"

D.B. and Dr. Chen laughed.

Eric cocked his crossbow and slid in a bolt. "Where are your prisoners, Dr. Chen?"

Dr. Chen gave Eric an angry look. "Why are you so interested in them?"

"I'm looking for somebody. They might know where he is."

"Who are you looking for?"

Eric and D.B. answered at the same time. Only their answers were very different.

"His son," D.B. said.

"Dirk Fallows," Eric said.

Eric and D.B. exchanged glances. He could see the bewilderment in her eyes, though he hoped she couldn't see the same thing in his own. He looked away, staring out over the garden, seeing the swollen green zucchinis, the plump red tomatoes.

Dirk Fallows. Is that what this was all about? Not Timmy at all? He had given himself such pure motives for every action: rescuing his son. But if revenge was all that drove him, was Tim really any better off with him than with Fallows?

"Let's go," Eric said.

Dr. Chen led them across the zoo, keeping the paths that she said the animals that were loose usually didn't bother coming near because there was no food.

As they walked, Dr. Chen and Spock in the lead, D.B. fell in beside Eric.

"He wouldn't even be asking," D.B. said.

"What?"

"Fallows. He wouldn't even be asking himself the questions you are."

Eric didn't look at her. "You don't know him."

"Don't I?" She gripped her choke collar tightly, her knuckles white under the pressure. "He's like the men who put this on me. I know men like that. I know."

Eric walked on without saying anything. Then he looked at her with a small smile. "When'd you get so damn wise."

"Always have been," she said. "You just never noticed."

"Hey, man, talk some sense into this lady."

"Yeah. Let us outta here."

Eric looked at the two men standing with their faces pressed up against the wire mesh. One was black, the other white. They wore chambray shirts and dungarees, the uniforms of navy men in active service. The badge on their sleeves showed two dolphins standing on either side of a submarine. The white man was big and beefy, with puffed jowls and tiny pinpoint eyes. He wore a petty officer's stripes. The black man was tall and thin and had to stoop slightly in the six-foot cage. He had only one chevron on his sleeve.

They were inside the Primate Propagation Center. The two men stared out at the four of them with a cold malignant gaze they were unsuccessful in concealing.

"What the fuck's going on?" the white petty officer asked.

"Trespassing," Eric said. "Didn't you read the signs? It's illegal."

The petty officer spat on the floor of the cage. "Shit, man, there ain't no more laws. Me and Washington here just got lost. We were hungry." He grinned, his lips pulling back to reveal square chunky teeth similar to Spock's. "Okay, maybe we was wrong coming in here to the little lady's private game reserve. We didn't know."

Eric looked at the black man. "What's your name?"

"Seaman Monroe Adams Washington." He shrugged and grinned. "My mama tried to cram as many presidents into my name as possible. My brother Lyndon's even worse off."

Eric smiled. "He in the navy too?"

"Marines. Figured they get all the chicks."

"Not all," the petty officer winked.

Eric inspected both men, pacing back and forth in front of the cage. "How long have you had them?" he asked Dr. Chen.

"Five fucking days!" the petty officer said. "We been cooped up in this pen for five days. We gotta piss and crap in a goddamn can that she don't empty but once a day. It's goddamn humiliating."

104

Eric turned to D.B. "Take Spock outside and wait."

"Will he go with me?" she asked Dr. Chen.

"Sure. Take his hand and lead him. If he gets restless, keep tickling him. He can take that for hours."

D.B. took the ape's hand. "Come on, Spock. Time to beam aboard." They left.

"Look it that," the petty officer said. "They let the goddamn ape go waltzing around while we stay locked up in a fucking cage."

"The ape," Dr. Chen said, "is a vegetarian. They don't eat animals."

Washington shook his head. "Look, lady, we know we made a mistake. We only want to get out of here and back to our home. We got family." He looked at Eric. "You look like you understand. Help us out, mister."

"Where's your home?" Eric asked.

"Well it used to be on board the *Dakota*. Slickest damn sub you ever seen. We were docked in San Diego for some repairs when the quakes hit. Ocean churned up so much it tore the sub in two like it was some toy you get out of a cereal box."

"Where do you live now?" Eric persisted.

"South," the petty officer. "That's all you need to know."

"Near Dirk Fallows' camp?"

"Who?" they both chorused.

"Corporal Dirk Fallows." Eric stepped closer to the cage. "He and his men are buying gold around here. I'm looking to peddle some."

Washington said, "Look, man, if it would help us any, I'd tell you about this Fallows. I'll tell you everything from birthplace to shoe size. But the truth is, we don't know the dude."

"Or anything about gold," the petty officer said. "Why would anybody be buying gold here? Don't make sense."

"Ours is not to reason why. Ours is just to make a profit."

Washington laughed. "He sounds like you, Bolinski."

Bolinski grinned wolfishly. "Yeah, well in Philly, ya gotta have a shark's instincts just to make it to the corner schoolhouse alive."

Eric didn't say anything for a while. He paced in front of their cage. He stopped in front of Bolinski, studying the huge muscular arms where his shirt was rolled up past the elbows. "You're looking a little pale, Bolinski. Not getting much sun down south lately?"

"Hey, pal, I looked a hell of a lot tanner before I got locked up in this brig."

"Yeah," Monroe chuckled, "even my tan is fading."

Eric shrugged. "I'd like to help you boys, I really would. But unless you can tell me where I can find Fallows, I can't do a thing. Take it easy, fellas." He started to walk out of the room, followed closely by Dr. Chen.

"Goddamn it, man, help us," Bolinski bellowed. "It's not our fault we don't know no Colonel Fallows. We were just hunting for food for our families. Shit, that's not a crime, even now."

Once outside, Eric pulled Dr. Chen aside. "What are you planning to do with them?"

"Let them go, I guess. I just held them long enough to see if they had any friends following. Guess not."

"Hold onto them one more day. Okay?"

She eyed him suspiciously. "Why? They're taking

106

up time and eating my food. They seem to be telling the truth. I'm sorry they don't know this Fallows man, but you can't punish them for that."

"Hold them," Eric said. "They're lying."

She shook her head. "I'm a pretty good judge of character, Mr. Ravensmith. I believe those two men. And since this is my compound, I'll decide who to detain and who not to."

Eric released the safety on his crossbow and bumped the arrow-end against Dr. Chen's chest. "If you're such a good judge of character, why is my finger on this trigger. Less than a pound's worth of pressure will make this zoo mine."

Dr. Chen did not back down. Her dark eyes bored into Eric's. "I know you can kill, Mr. Ravensmith. I recognize the look. But I was hasty in my earlier condemnation, letting my grief for my father interfere with my judgment. Yes, you could kill me. But you won't. I believe your young companion. You want to find your son. You won't do that here."

Eric flicked the safety on and lowered the bow. "You don't bluff so easily yourself, Doctor."

"Wendy," she said with a relieved sigh. She offered her hand. Eric shook it. It was warm, the skin calloused from gardening.

"Maybe you are right about me," Eric said. "But you are wrong about them. They know something."

"Male intuition?" she smiled.

"Evidence. You notice their uniforms? A little soiled, but no tears or serious wear. They're fairly new."

"They could have had extra uniforms."

"Look how pale Bolinski is. People in California all have tans, only these days it's not from lying around the beach or playing tennis. It's from hunting or gardening or building. He's too pale, and it's not from natural skin pigmentation."

Dr. Chen started to offer an explanation, then stopped. "What else?"

"I referred to Fallows as Corporal Fallows. Later Bolinski called him Colonel Fallows, which is correct."

Dr. Chen absently picked a lock of her straight black hair and began chewing on it. "What does that add up to?"

"Unanswered questions. I intend to find out the answers tonight."

"How?"

Eric's smile was cold and flat. "You don't want to know."

11

The rain came suddenly. At first it was a pounding rain, harsh and almost vengeful, but after an hour it calmed to a gentle pelting.

"That's the only blessing out of all this," Wendy Chen said, staring out the window. "California finally gets enough rain. Something about the Halo, I suspect."

"At this rate," Eric said, "within a year or two vegetation will have reclaimed most of the land."

"And insects," D.B. complained, swatting at something flying around her face.

Wendy pulled her hair back and tied a hunk of rope around it, forming a long black pony tail that hung down to her buttocks. "The point is, in a couple years, people will have to overcome whatever fears and differences they have to form little pocket societies, like the city-states of ancient Greece. The rest of the state will be a tropical jungle. That's when I'll release the animals."

Eric smiled. "Let them go forth, two by two, and be fruitful and multiply."

"Okay, maybe it sounds a trifle pretentious. But what's wrong with a little Eden?"

"Paradise regained?" Eric said. "It's been tried."

"Not by me." She pressed her hand against the window, watched the glass fog up around her warm flesh. "You're probably right. It is crazy."

"But nice crazy," D.B. said.

Spock was in the corner of the room arranging thick shaggy rugs over a large tractor tire. He worked slowly, but meticulously, shifting and tugging the carpets until they were just right.

"What's he doing?" D.B. asked.

"Making his bed. It's his own design. He had a mattress once, but he tore it apart within an hour. Actually, that arrangement is remarkably comfortable."

"Yeah?" D.B. went over and stood next to Spock. "Mind if I try it out, Spock?"

Spock looked at her, puzzled. Then he looked at Wendy. Wendy signed to him while talking to D.B. "I'm telling him you like his bed."

Spock signed back and Wendy and Eric laughed.

"What'd he say?" D.B. asked.

"He says it's his bed," Eric said. "And that you should go find your own."

D.B. poked Spock playfully. "You little punk."

"How sharper than a serpent's tooth is an ungrateful ape," Eric said.

"You'll find it's not all games and tickling with Spock," Wendy said. "He's like a child, stubborn and petulant and moody. He requires an enormous amount of attention."

"Doesn't he play with Madonna?" D.B. asked.

"Oh yes. They play for hours. And the amazing thing is he has been teaching her Ameslan. He's taught her seven signs outside those that I taught her. But he wants favorite-child status. Special privileges."

"What do you do then?"

"The same as with any child. Discipline. Like now. He's acting this way because we aren't paying any attention to him. So we'll leave. It's time he got some sleep anyway."

Eric nodded. "It's time we all got some sleep."

The three of them started for the door. Immediately, Spock plopped onto the floor and began making a mournful whoo-whoo sound.

"What's he doing?" D.B. asked.

"Crying. Apes don't shed tears."

The sound continued.

"Aren't you going to do something?"

Wendy shook her head. "He'll stop. I pamper him enough."

They walked down the hall, the whoo-whoo sound echoing around them. That and the sad patter of rain was too much for D.B. She stopped. "I can't stand it. Look, I don't want to screw up your scientific experiments or anything, but can I stay with him a little longer? I mean, he won't suddenly go nuts or anything, will he?"

Wendy looked at Eric, who shrugged and said, "She's always been a sucker for stray apes."

"Okay. You can stay with him. He can be rough playing, so be careful. Just in case you get sleepy, you may want to stick a few of the stuffed alligator dolls around you. He won't come near you then."

D.B. laughed. "Come on."

"Really. He's afraid of alligators, even though he's never seen one, never even been near the reptile house. But I've shown him pictures and it makes him very frightened. So I use little alligator dolls from the gift shop and stick them in places I don't want him to go. It works."

D.B. hurried back toward Spock's room. She called back without turning her head. "You two have fun. Maybe you can find a good book to read together or give each other pop quizzes." Her laughter drowned out even Spock's moaning. They heard her unlatch Spock's door. His moaning stopped altogether.

"Well," Wendy said, unbuttoning her blouse. "Are we going to make love or what?"

Her home was a trailer just behind the Animal Care Center. They walked through the warm rain, her blouse open, the large drops bursting against her smooth dark skin. She wore a white bra that had a tan sweat line under each cup. Somehow, that thin discolored line was more erotic to Eric than the sight of her breasts or thoughts of what they would be doing. In those tan lines were hours, months, of hard work, laboring to keep this place functioning. To keep the animals alive. Not for any personal gain or profit, but for some wacky dream about populating the encroaching California jungle with animals. He admired her determination. And that was the strongest aphrodisiac of all.

They stepped into her trailer. The inside was spartan. There was a single bed, a battered old dresser, a radio/cassette player, a desk scattered with scientific data about the apes. Taped on the wall was a map of the zoo with Post-it notes slapped here and there with details for where she planned to improve the place.

"Homey," Eric said.

She shrugged out of her khaki shirt. She began unbuttoning his shirt.

112

"Not much on small talk, huh?" he said.

"You want to talk or you want to screw?"

"You pick that up in Cambridge?"

"I picked it up living alone here for almost a year." She stood on her toes and pressed her lips against his. They were slightly chapped from the sun and tasted a little salty, but they also had a moist sweetness that drew Eric closer. He pulled her tight against him, her hard body feeling weightless in his arms.

After a minute she pulled back, her eyes open, looking at him. "I understand American men prefer their women passive."

"Some do," Eric said.

"You?"

Eric kissed her over each eye. "You want to arm wrestle first?"

She laughed. "I have a better idea."

"I'm all ears."

"I hope not." She unfastened her bra and shook it off. Then she pulled off her safari shorts. Underneath she wore men's boxer shorts. "All I could find," she explained.

Eric watched her closely as he undressed. Her movements were not shy or consciously sexy. She disrobed as simply as if she were alone preparing for bed. He liked that.

She stepped out of the boxer shorts and stood next to the bed wearing only her blue Rebock aerobic shoes. "Sometimes Spock gets in here and breaks something," she said, "then tries to hide it by sweeping it under the bed. I leave the shoes for last so I don't step on any stray pieces." She sat on the edge of the bed and pulled off one shoe. A ring of dirt circled the ankle, just above where the shoe had been. From working in the garden, Eric realized. "I used to take aerobics classes every evening before the quakes. Funny, but my cadiovascular system feels stronger now than it ever did then." She kicked off her other shoe and had a matching ring of dirt. She licked her finger and rubbed at the dirt. It did little good. She laughed. "Well, what did you expect? A virgin princess?"

Eric stripped off the rest of his clothes while she sat cross-legged in the middle of the bed. She looked so small naked, that he was aware of his own broad chest and heavily veined arms as he removed the last of his clothing.

She leaned back onto the bed and patted the space next to her. "I know it's a small bed, but you'll fit. Spock and I have both fit before."

She saw an expression flicker across Eric's face.

"I don't mean *that* way. Just sitting."

"I didn't say anything."

"No, but you were curious. I know I would be if I were you. Lonely woman living happily alone with apes. When real men come in she throws them in cages. Sounds screwy to me."

Eric stretched out beside her, wrapping an arm around her waist. Her toes grazed his shins.

"It's just that I didn't want sex with just anyone. Not that I'm looking for anything long term. I just wanted it to be nice, the way I remember it."

Eric kissed her. Their lips ground against each other, tongues rubbing against each other like cats. His hand cupped her buttocks and pulled her closer. Her hand slipped between them and held his penis tight. He could feel it growing even harder in her grasp.

"Let's just get the suspense over with," she urged. "We can go for fireworks later."

114

Eric didn't mind occasional hasty sex. He remembered how often he'd met Annie home for lunch for what she called her One-hour Workout. She had it timed perfectly: ten minutes to drive home, five minutes for chit-chat and undressing, ten minutes for sex, five minutes for washing and redressing, twenty minutes for lunch together, and ten minutes to drive back to work. Sometimes they skipped lunch altogether.

Usually he preferred a longer, more relaxed encounter. He wanted the tenderness, which was rarer than food or ammunition.

Wendy grabbed Eric around his waist and rolled him over on top of her. She spread her legs and guided him inside, hooking her legs over his hips before he got a deep breath. Now she was arching her pelvis toward him, her hip bones bumping his with a rhythmic grace. Soon he was matching her, thrust for thrust. Her movements quickened, became more insistent. Greedy. Her breathing was ragged, gasping. Eric felt both their bodies slicken with sweat. Her ankles slid down his hips to the backs of his thighs.

She spoke softly in Chinese and he answered her in Chinese. It was nothing specific, no vows. Just encouragement, gentle thoughts of pleasure. An image of Annie fought into his mind and he pushed it away.

Suddenly she tensed, her body slapping against his, her arms curled around his neck. Her hips were off the bed, pushed against his as hard as they could go. Her face clenched, the eyes disappearing into lines of passion. Her mouth was open and she pulled his lips to hers, pushing her tongue into his mouth. As she came, he felt a hum at the back of her throat travelling along her tongue and into his mouth. It was a thrilling sensation. He came seconds after her, his body quivering with each spasm.

"I feel guilty," she said, huddled against Eric's side. Her fingernails grated through his chest hair.

"Why?"

"I thought of my boyfriend just as I came. I didn't want to, but I did."

Eric smiled. "We all have our ghosts."

"You don't understand. Gregory survived the quakes with me. The Zoo had let me keep my trailer here while I worked with Spock and Madonna. Gregory had been a photojournalist doing a story on my work. That's how we met. Anyway, when the quakes hit, a lot of people here were killed, not from the actual quake, but trampling each other on their way to the parking lot. Gregory made his way here to find me and I convinced him to stay here and help me rebuild the zoo. He did." She rolled away from him, tucking her knees up.

He ran his hand along her arm. "And then?"

"He was killed. The quake had freed two Brazilian jaguars. They'd been killing and eating some of the other animals so Greg and I tried to trap them. Only they got Greg first. He was dead by the time I arrived, though while they were feeding off him, I managed to net them both. They're back in their cages now."

"And you had to bury Greg."

"Not exactly." She turned around to face Eric. "Before I got my garden going, I had to rely on the zoo's storeroom to feed all these animals. You have no idea how much they eat and how scientifically controlled it is. Anyway, we knew it wouldn't take long for us to run out of food, so Greg and I supplemented their diet."

Eric lifted himself onto his elbow. "The bodies."

"Yes. We dragged in as many as we could from the parking lot and adjacent areas, chopped them up, and fed them to the animals. We debated the whole thing for two days before noticing that the other animals on the outside were already starting to nibble away on them. That convinced us." She looked at Eric. "When Greg died it was just a natural extension of what we'd already done. I fed him to the Asian lions. It's what I'd have expected him to do if it were me."

Eric flopped back down onto the pillow.

She sat up. "I'm terrible, aren't I?"

Eric didn't answer for a while. He thought about all that he'd done since the world changed, all that he'd seen people doing to each other. What had Wendy Chen done so awful? Made use of what resources were available to keep lives going. Perhaps the outside world would never understand, but then they didn't have to. They could make judgments from their tables at restaurants while waiters stuffed doggie bags with leftovers.

She pounded her fist into her pillow. "Sometimes I think I'm really insane. All this work and anguish over some cockeyed notion of turning this wasteland into paradise."

Eric pulled her on top of him. "We could use a little paradise around here."

They kissed. Slowly they explored each other. Lips, fingers, skin, and hair touched and mixed in one long movement. This time they went for fireworks.

Hours later, as Wendy slept quietly next to him, Eric slipped out of bed, dressed, picked up his crossbow, and took the keys from her pants. He eased out of the trailer without a sound. It took him less than five minutes to cross the zoo to the Primate

Propogation Center where Seaman Washington and Petty Officer Bolinski were imprisoned.

"Well, gentlemen," he said, standing in front of their cage, his crossbow pointed at them. "It's truth or consequences time."

12

Eric dangled the key to their cage. "Want to go for a walk, boys?"

Bolinski eyed Eric skeptically. "What do you want?"

"Freedom. Freedom for my fellow man."

"For a price?"

Eric shrugged. "There's always a price on freedom."

Washington sat at the back of the cage. His shoes were five feet away. His socks were balled up and he was lobbing them toward the empty shoes in a makeshift game of basketball. He tossed his sock. It dropped neatly into the shoe. He looked at Eric. "Don't jerk us around, man. You gonna let us out, fine. Do it. You gonna jerk us around, get lost."

Eric smiled broadly. "Just had to be sure." He inserted the key and unlocked the cage. He pulled open the door. "Last stop before Trenton."

The two men scrambled out of the cage, Washington grabbing his shoes and socks on the way. Now that they were out, he sat on the ground and pulled them onto his feet.

"Who are you?" Bolinski asked. His tiny eyes were fixed on Eric like barnacles.

"I'm the guy who just let you out."

"Why? What do you want? And don't give me none of that freedom bullshit."

Eric's face went hard. "Fallows sent me."

The two men exchanged looks. Petty Officer Bolinski sneered, his upper lip curling to reveal lower teeth so crowded some were wedged in sideways like packed subway riders. "We already told you, we don't know no Fallows."

"Suit yourself," Eric said. "He sent me here to get you out and bring you back. He's a little pissed at you boys for screwing everything up. But maybe I've got the wrong guys. There must be plenty of salt and pepper teams with submarine uniforms." He motioned with his crossbow. "Back inside, fellas. I've got to keep hunting."

"No, wait," Washington said. He finished tying his shoes and stood up. A splash of freckles marked his forehead. His hair had a hint of red beneath the black curls. "We'll go with you."

Eric lowered his crossbow a little, his finger drifting from the trigger. He knew that's what they were waiting for. If Washington kept talking and Bolinksi began inching to Eric's side, he knew he was right about them. Then there would be only one thing to do.

"What about the women?" Washington asked, grinning at Eric.

"What about them?" Eric said.

"Shit, man, we're talking about women! You want the chink, fine. I like 'em young anyway. I'll take the skinny kid in the dog collar. I mean, whatever is right —"

As he talked, Eric could sense Bolinski's movements, slight, almost imperceptible. Mostly he was shifting his body weight, balancing himself for leverage. But he was hesitating, unsure. Eric decided to make it easy for him. He switched the crossbow to his left hand and used his right hand to scratch the back of his head.

Bolinksi lunged.

Eric could tell from the body position what form the attack would take before it happened. Nothing fancy. Bolinski was no martial arts expert. He was the kind of man who'd relied on sheer size and brute strength all his life. He would simply try to hammer Eric with his meaty fists.

Eric relaxed his shoulder and hip muscles just as Bolinski lunged. The blow connected with Eric's left arm, but he allowed the force of the punch to swivel him on his hips, something like a weather vane. Still, his shoulder ached from the impact.

Now Washington was grabbing for him too.

Eric did just as he'd planned. He pushed himself backward against the cage door and slid to the ground. While the two men shifted their positions of attack to accommodate, Eric brought the crossbow up, thumbed the safety off, and fired a short lethal bolt into Bolinski's chest. The arrow drilled so deep that only part of the feather cluster was still visible in his chest.

Bolinski staggered backward a step, dropped to one knee, flexed his hands into claws, and reached for Eric. From his seated position, Eric snapped out a sidekick that planted his foot right on the tip of the arrow, driving it further into the petty officer's chest. Bolinski toppled with a groan, spoke three words in Russian, and died.

13

"Hey, kid. Come here."

Tim looked around. The huge fire in the middle of the camp sent some tendrils of light throughout the campsite. Enough to see the three men sitting in front of their tent swigging on a bottle of Southern Comfort they'd taken on a raid last week. They were laughing and poking each other, but Tim could tell they were in an angry mood. The one in the middle, Judd, waved at Tim to join them.

"C'mon over, kid. Join the party." Judd gulped from the bottle, wiped his mouth with the back of his hand, then licked his own hand. "Don't wanna waste a fuckin' drop," he snickered. The others laughed drunkenly.

Tim kept going. He'd come out of his tent only to relieve himself in the woods. He wasn't interested in whatever these men had to say, especially Judd, whose arrogance was well known among the men. He was only barely tolerated by Fallows.

Tim passed a thick pine tree on his way back to his tent. A sudden thunk behind him caused him to turn to see the handle of Judd's knife wobbling in the trunk of the pine tree. Tim saw Judd standing, his body twisted into the stance of a man's who'd just thrown a knife. The booze had washed away the frozen smirk that usually highlighted his narrow face. Now all that was left was a cruel grimace, a malevolence in the eyes that marked every one of Fallows' followers, but seemed magnified in Judd's eyes, as if viewed under thick glasses.

"Even genius brats like you gotta talk to the common folk some times, kid," Judd said. "Just to see how real people live." Judd drank again. When he lowered the bottle, back was his grinning smirk. He winked and waved at Tim like they were old chums. "C'mon, Tim. Have a drop or two with us."

Tim decided it was better to go along for a few minutes than to cause any trouble. He plucked Judd's knife from the pine tree and walked over to their tent.

"Yes?" he said.

"Ever have drink before? I mean hard stuff."

Tim shook his head.

"Here. Try it." He offered the bottle.

Tim didn't take it.

"Oops," Judd said. He took the bottle back, wiped the bottle opening on his shirt, and offered it again. "There, that's better. More hygienic."

"Hygienic," Dyson, one of Judd's buddies, said. "I like the sound of that."

"If not the practice of it," Judd said. All three men laughed.

Tim turned to go. Judd's large hand fell on his shoulder, holding him back.

"Not so fast, little brother. I mean, you are our little brother, aren't you. Colonel Fallows is our father, and you've become his . . . His what?" He winked at Dyson, but Dyson didn't respond. It was one thing to tease the kid, but to say anything about Colonel Fallows was asking for trouble.

Judd didn't seem to be afraid. "I mean, the good colonel did give you your own damn tent, didn't he?

I've got to bunk with these two crawfish and you've got your own fuckin' tent." He looked around at Dyson and Bechler. Both men seemed suddenly sober. "I mean, look at these two. Ever seen two men more disgusting. Dyson here jacks off in the middle of the night when he thinks we're asleep."

Dyson started angrily to his feet. "Wait a min—"

Judd swung the bottle of Southern Comfort around and cracked Dyson across the face. Dyson's cheekbone swelled to a large blue knob and the shattered glass plowed three deep furrows across his jaw. He fell unconscious to the ground.

At the sound of breaking glass, some of the other men in the camp looked over. Their expressions were bored, indifferent, only mildly curious at the break in routine. They watched, but no one interfered.

"Bechler here is worse," Judd chuckled. "Son of a bitch farts in his sleep. By morning the tent smells like a latrine. Right, Bechler?" He looked sharply at Bechler.

Bechler grinned. "That's true enough. Never could hold my gas."

"But you, runt," Judd said, pointing at Tim, though Tim stood almost as tall at six feet as Judd. "You get a tent all to yourself. What are you doin' for it, kid, suckin' Fallows off?"

Tim straightened at the accusation, feeling his hand tightening around the knife handle he was still holding. Anger burned deep in his stomach and the tops of his ears. He wanted to do something, not just because of what Judd said but because he was tired of having to take crap from everyone. At first they had all mistreated him, taking their cue from Fallows. The scars from the knife cuts and cigarette burns he'd endured as punishment back then still pocked the skin of his arms and neck. Later, when

125

Fallows showed more open regard, the men had begrudgingly imitated their leader. But the hostility and resentment from everyone was evident. Only their fear of Fallows kept them from displaying any outward signs. Until now.

"How old are you, boy?" Judd asked.

"Thirteen. Almost fourteen."

Judd held up his hands in mock-awe. "Wow. Thirteen fuckin' years. You know how old I am? Thirty-six. Yeah, thirty-six years old and still sleeping with roommates in a tent that smells like the devil's asshole. That seem right to you?"

Tim said nothing.

"I mean, does that seem right that a guy my age should be penned up with these two slobs while some thirteen-almost-fourteen-year-old punk gets his own goddamn tent?" He took a step toward Tim.

Tim didn't flinch. "Perhaps you should ask Colonel Fallows."

Judd lashed out and slapped Tim across the cheek. The force spun Tim backward to the ground. "Maybe I should just claim you were trying to escape and kill you right now. That would leave an opening for your tent."

Tim's face stung. The slap had caught him wrong and he clamped his jaw together on his tongue. He cold taste the dull metallic flavor of blood in his mouth. He looked up at Judd. "If you're going to kill me, then do it. Don't talk me to death."

Judd swung again with a backhand slap that snapped Tim's head around. The big man laughed. "You asked for it, kid." He glanced at Bechler. "Didn't he ask for it? Huh?"

"He asked for it," Bechler quickly agreed.

Tim stayed on the ground. His anger was so great that his skin seemed to shrink, tightening around his bones and muscles like the skin of a tomato. He realized that the angrier he got, the less afraid he was. And he was afraid. He'd seen what Judd could do, had watched him on several raids using those throwing knives of his, picking a target area—head, throat, heart—and betting with someone if he could kill some victim who was running away.

"You think you're one of us?" Judd said, standing over Tim. "You think 'cause Fallows drags you along, that makes you tough?" Judd's face contorted into pure hate. "Maybe if you do for me what you do for Fallows, I'll let you live." He unzipped his fly. "Well?"

"Jesus, man," Bechler said. "You'd better cool it, Judd."

"Or what?" Judd snapped. "Daddy Fallows gonna spank?"

"Suit yourself," Bechler said, jumping to his feet and jogging off.

Judd's hand seemed to scratch at his thigh and then suddenly there was a flat throwing knife in his hand just like the one he'd tossed at the tree. His arm swooped down and the blade whirled through the air picking up red flickers from the campfire as it spun. It stuck in the back of Bechler's right thigh and he let out a yowl of pain.

The others in camp continued to watch. No one interfered.

Except Fallows.

"What's going on here?" Fallows said, stepping out of his tent. He was smiling, his teeth large and white. He brushed his hand over his close-cropped white hair that came to a sharp widow's peak over his forehead. "Having a party, Judd?"

Judd looked frightened at first, like a child caught with his hand in his father's wallet. But then he turned defiant, stiffening a little as he felt everyone's eyes on him. "Yeah, Colonel, I'm having a party."

"And you didn't invite me? How rude."

Judd seemed confused by Fallows' calm smiling demeanor. His right hand passed near his thigh again where his secret pockets held several more throwing knives.

Tim watched without moving. Fallows kept walking closer, but he didn't even look at Tim. Maybe he's angry at me, Tim thought, and is going to punish me. It was hard to tell with Fallows. His moods didn't seem to relate to anything outside himself.

"You have something to say, Judd?" Fallows asked. He stopped walking. Tim sat on the ground between the two men.

"Yeah, I got something to say. I say this is between me and the kid and you have no business sticking up for him. If he rides with us and eats a share of what we take, then he ought to fight with us too. So far all he's done is moon around. He's never killed or captured anyone. Yet he wears new clothes, eats good food, sleeps alone in a tent."

Fallows looked at Tim, brushing his hand over his hair again. "Well, kid, he's got you there." And with that Fallows turned and walked back into his tent.

Tim sat on the ground, alone.

Judd's grin twisted across his face like a strand of barbed wire. "So much for protection, punk. Now, where were we? Oh yeah." His grin broadened as he pulled his zipper the rest of the way down. "Time for a little late night snack, boy."

Tim felt the fear again. The coldness in his stomach. The dryness in his mouth. His hands shivered.

"Tell ya what," Judd said. "I'm gonna give you a chance. Man to man. I'm gonna let you go for your gun, just like in them cowboy movies. Like in *The*

Magnificent Seven, when James Coburn draws against that other guy. Only Jimmy's got a knife and the other guy's got a gun. Remember that?"

"Neville Brand," Tim said.

"Huh?"

"That's who played the other cowboy."

"Who gives a shit?"

Tim felt a little better. He'd been able to speak despite his fear. He'd told Judd something he didn't know, something meaningless, but it was something. And that little bit of useless trivia made him feel slightly more confident. It made Judd seem less invincible. If only this were a trivia duel, Tim thought, I'd kick his ass. He smiled to himself. That was something his father would have said. But it was good he could still laugh. His hands weren't shaking anymore.

"What's the matter, kid?" Judd asked. "Not feeling too chatty, huh? Scared? Tell you what, I'm gonna let you unsnap your holster flap first. Go ahead."

Tim dropped the knife he still held. Slowly he moved his hand toward his holster, his fingers unsnapping the flap.

"That better?" Judd looked around at the others who stared across the fire at them. "I'll even go one better, kid. I'll turn my back." He turned away from Tim, though he still looked at him over his shoulder. "Now, before I look away, let's get the rules straight. Once I turn my head, you're on your own. You can pull your fancy gun out and start shooting. All I'll have are my knives."

Tim looked at the back of Judd's pants. Long narrow pockets lined the backs and sides of each thigh. A Velcro flap held the knives in place. Tim calculated how long it would take for Judd to pull the knife out, turn, and throw. Surely he could pull his gun quicker.

"Ready?" Judd asked.

But he'd just seen how quickly Judd had managed to nail Bechler in the leg. It had happened so fast Tim hadn't even seen Judd pull out the knife.

"Ready, kid?" Judd repeated.

Tim nodded.

Pulling open the flap would take a moment, so would drawing out the gun. The safety was on, that would take a fraction of a second too. Aiming wouldn't take long, neither would pulling the trigger. But add them up. Tim didn't know.

"Here we go," Judd said, his head slowly swiveling away.

Oddly, Tim found himself wondering, not what his father would do in this situation, but what Fallows would do. After all, it was Fallows who had beaten Eric so far, who had kidnapped Tim and survived every raid and provided the best available goods for his men. Who would know better?

"Go!" Judd said.

Tim watched Judd's right hand swing back, the thumb extended, digging under the Velcro, prying the flap apart. The index finger and thumb pinching the black blade, pulling it free.

Tim's instincts were to go for his gun, to scuttle back as far away from Judd as possible as he fired. That made sense. Increasing the range would give the gun the advantage.

But Tim didn't even go for his gun.

What happened next was something he'd heard about, but never understood. Something his father had told him about, something Big Bill Tenderwolf had described, something Fallows had tried to explain. They had each talked about a moment when your brain gave itself over to the body. It wasn't instinct, because it told him to go for the gun. It was some primal pulsing at the back of the brain, a black box that released a warm inky fluid that washed over Tim in an instant. And suddenly he was moving, doing things over which he had no say, no control. Logic was dead.

He did not go for the gun. He did not back away.

Instead he grabbed the knife that'd he'd dropped. And as Judd spun around, one of his flat black throwing knives raised high over his head ready for launching, Tim leaned forward, toward Judd, and plunged the knife straight into Judd's open fly.

Judd screamed like no one Tim had ever heard scream. Judd's knife dropped to the ground as both his hands went toward his crotch.

Tim drove the knife deeper, holding on tightly as Judd clawed at his hands.

"You little fucker," Judd rasped, his clawing becoming weaker. He dropped to his knees, face level now with Tim. But still Tim clutched the knife, pressing it forward, though it could go no deeper.

Judd toppled over, dead. His eyes stared at the dirt.

Still Tim would not release the knife. He couldn't. It was as if he had plugged into some electrical socket and nothing but pure energy was surging through his body. Even Judd's warm blood oozing over his fingers was like an invigorating salve. It was like the old beliefs Big Bill used to tell him about how killing an enemy gave you his strength. That's what Tim felt, like he had more strength and power than his body could contain.

Finally, Tim let go of the knife and stood up.

The men around the fire looked at him as blandly as if he'd just stepped on an ant. One of them took a swig from his canteen and said, "Your mess, kid.

You clean it up."

Tim smiled. Despite their hardened gazes, he could tell they respected him and even, a little, feared him. Now he belonged. After all these months, he belonged. He knew now what they felt on those raids, the sense of power, almost invulnerability. What would his father say? Tim wondered. Surely he must have felt it too, in Vietnam. Yet Tim knew his father would disapprove of these feelings, would try to stop them. And right now Tim didn't want them to stop. Ever.

He looked over at Fallows' tent, saw the flap move slightly. Had Fallows been watching? He must have, Tim realized. That made him feel good. Proud.

"Hey," Bechler yelled, struggling to stand on his wounded leg. "Anybody gonna give me a hand?"

No one moved. Tim looked at the others, at Bechler. He smiled and walked back to his tent.

14

Eric nudged Bolinski's dead body with his foot. "More food for the zoo animals." He turned to Washington. "What about you? Want to be on tomorrow's menu?"

Washington shook his head. "No way, man."

"Good, then let's get going."

"Sure, man. Whatever you say. Where to?"

Eric looked disappointed as he reloaded his crossbow. "Fallows said you guys were stupid, but he didn't say *this* stupid."

Washington didn't respond. Eric aimed the crossbow at him. Washington raised his hands and backpedaled a couple of steps.

Eric stooped over Bolinski's body and pulled the bolt out. He wiped the blood on Bolinski's blue shirt and shoved it back into the quiver at his waist. "Bolinski was your commander, therefore he's responsible for this screw-up. Fallows instructed me to make sure he was punished." Eric grinned.

"He had no right!" Washington shouted angrily. Then, aware that he may have said too much, he laughed. "Bolinski may have been a fool, but he was an okay dude, man."

Eric spoke in Russian. "Now he is a dead dude."

"What is that? Pig Latin?"

Eric lifted the crossbow to his shoulder and aimed down the runner, lining up the bolt's point with Washington's chest. Again he spoke in Russian. "Fallows said if I thought you were going to screw up this operation any more, I should fix you too. Well?"

Washington stared for a minute, his eyes studying Eric, calculating. Finally he let out a deep weary sigh. He nodded at Eric, answering in Russian. "Let's go."

"You first," Eric said.

They hiked through the zoo, Eric watchful for any stray animals. He let Washington lead the way since he had no idea where they were going. Except back to Fallows.

So far it was working. Killing Bolinski had convinced Washington that Eric was indeed sent by Fallows, though Eric still didn't know what the connection was between the two Soviets and Fallows. Nor did he know why two Russians were dressed in U.S. navy uniforms, or why they were posing as Americans.

"Your American is impressive," Eric said.

"Better than your Russian."

"Six-week crash course in the service. Tourist stuff mostly."

Washington smiled. "Lingo, baby. Jive. That's what I speak."

"You learn it in spy school?"

"Spy school?" he laughed. "Shit, I learned it at UCLA. I'm South African. Zulu, to be exact. I was a teenager fighting the Afrikaners' apartheid in my country with small acts of terrorism. Well, more like vandalism. Slashing tires and such of white businessmen. My father disapproved, naturally, being a member of the Colored Persons Representative Council. Anyway, my underground activities were noticed and I was given money to help organize other youths."

"KGB," Eric said.

"Yes, though I didn't know that at the time. Not that it would have mattered. They were doing something to help our cause."

Eric didn't want to ask too many questions, questions that someone sent by Fallows would know the answers to. Like what he was doing here. He'd have to stick to the personal chatter, pick up what he could.

They came to the outer wall. Washington pointed to the barbed wire across the top. "We'd cut through that coming in. She must've replaced it."

"I'll boost you up," Eric said. "Throw your shirt over the wire."

"Why me, man?"

Eric held up the crossbow. "Because I've got this."

Washington nodded. "Right."

Eric leaned the crossbow against the wall, laced his fingers together into a stirrup, and lifted Washington up onto the wall. Eric dusted off his hands and looked up. Washington was perched ten feet above him.

"Okay," Eric said, slinging his crossbow over his shoulder. "Give me your hand." He reached up.

Washington smiled. "Blow it out your ass, honky." And suddenly he leaped over the barbed wire and jumped down on the other side of the wall.

"Damn!" Eric said. He had thought killing Bolinski had put a big enough scare into Washington. Not so.

Eric ran back twenty feet from the wall, tightened the bow to his back, and ran full-speed for the wall. Three feet from the wall he jumped up, arching his back and extending his hands. Ten feet. The height of a basketball rim. All those days playing one-on-one with Big Bill, dribbling around him for his patented reverse lay-up. Jumping for the rim between games while Big Bill rested and sipped beers. His fingertips could feel the rust flakes where he barely grazed the bottom of the rim.

Eric's fingers caught the top of the wall, hooked over the edge by the first joints of the knuckles. His feet scrambled for purchase on the wall while his fingers pulled him up by inches. Then in one great effort, he was on top.

Washington was running through the dark, dodging left and right as he made for the deserted highway. Eric shouldered the crossbow, followed his zig-zagging for a few seconds, then squeezed the trigger. The bolt shooshed through the night and stabbed into the ground inches from Washington's running feet.

"Next one's in your leg," Eric shouted.

Washington kept running.

"Unless I miss and hit your back."

Washington stopped.

Eric stepped carefully over the barbed wire and jumped down from the wall. He reloaded his crossbow and jogged toward Washington.

"I had to try," Washington shrugged when Eric arrived.

"Why? Fallows and your people are on the same side, right?"

"An uneasy alliance." Washington pulled the arrow out of the ground and handed it to Eric. "But you are only guessing, aren't you, Mr. Ravensmith?"

Eric showed no response.

Washington continued. "I know who you are. Bolinski and I suspected. We have heard a great deal

136

about you since arriving here. The Warlord, isn't it?" When Eric didn't answer, Washington continued. "The locals have stories, exaggerations no doubt, but after seeing you at work, perhaps not."

"Why did you come with me?"

"Why not? I figured it was better to try to escape from you than be locked indefinitely in that cage. You were right about one thing, eventually Fallows or my people would have sent somebody. Bolinski and I were idiots to enter that place, selfishly looking for fresh meat. We had been scouting and Bolinski convinced me it would be nothing more than poaching a bird or two." Washington sighed. "So now you will kill me unless I tell you what Russians are doing in your precious California."

"No," Eric said.

Washington raised an eyebrow in surprise.

"But I will kill you if you don't take me to Fallows' camp."

"Then it is true. About your son. That boy is yours."

"You've seen Tim?"

Washington nodded. "With Fallows. He seems quiet, withdrawn."

Eric felt an aching in his chest. It must be what a man dying of thirst feels when he can smell the fresh water over the next dune. Eric gestured for Washington to lead the way and the tall black man started walking. Eric didn't think about the Russians or what they were doing here. He thought only of Tim. And Fallows. The rest was none of his business.

Now that Washington knew for sure who Eric was, he seemed even more talkative, almost friendly. "After a couple years of pranks, I became frustrated. The KGB financed my schooling here at UCLA, hoping I would come back and eventually be able to

137

join the government. But things move slowly in South Africa. Meantime, they recruited me for this special assignment. They needed people who could convince the locals we were Americans. Bolinski, now he learned his American in spy school. I thought he overdid the bad grammar myself, but—"

Three muffled pops sounded, like balloons breaking. Eric dove to the ground. When he looked up he saw Washington leaning against a tree, three large holes in his chest. Slowly he slid down the trunk until a broken branch hooked on one of the holes in his back and held him suspended there.

"Next shot takes your head, Eric," a voice called. The voice came from above, from someone perched sniper-style in a tree. Considering the darkness, the gunman had to have a night-scope.

Eric tossed away his crossbow and stood up, hands on top of his head.

Three men came crashing through the brush, each carrying automatic weapons. They grabbed Eric roughly, one of them jerking Eric's arms behind his back and slapping handcuffs on his wrists.

A minute later a lanky Vietnamese man carrying a rifle fixed with a night-scope sauntered in. He walked over to Washington's body, poked the chest with the muzzle of his Weatherby Mark V rifle. Blood dabbed the metal tip. He nodded at one of the other men. "Strip the body and bring the clothing back with you."

The man slung his M-16 over his shoulder, unhooked Washington's body from the tree trunk, and began pulling off the clothes.

The Vietnamese man walked up to Eric, a sly grin on his face. "Hello, Eric."

"Hello, Nhu."

"Surprised to see me?"

Eric shook his head. "Wherever Fallows goes, his cronies are sure to follow."

"He's waiting for you, Eric."

"Looks like the waiting is over. For both of us."

Book Three:

WAR BUDDIES

Many sensible things banished from high life find an asylum among the mob.
                              Herman Melville

15

"Hey. Wait up, guys." D.B. fastened the last button of her blouse as she ran after Wendy and Spock. They were marching toward the Primate Propogation Center. "What's the hurry?" she said as she caught up to them. She gave Spock a quick tickle in the ribs and a pat on the head. Spock raised his hairy arms for more tickling.

Wendy kept walking. Spock ambled beside her, swinging forward on his knuckles.

D.B. noticed for the first time that Wendy was carrying a hacksaw and a hatchet. "What's up?"

"Work."

"Yeah, I heard of that stuff. Causes cancer." D.B. smiled, but Wendy's eyes stayed solemn and straight ahead. Okay, a little curt, D.B. thought, but hey, maybe she just wasn't a morning person. Eric was pretty grouchy in the mornings too. Sometimes they didn't speak at all until lunch. "I didn't hear you come for Spock."

"You were still asleep. I didn't want to disturb you."

"Thanks. That was the best sleep I've had in months. Something about having a friendly gorilla in the room made me feel safe."

"Sometimes it's better than having a man sleep

143

over."

D.B. gave her a look. "Yeah?"

Wendy shook her head. "I don't mean sexually."

"No, of course. I just, well, was, you know, curious . . ."

Wendy laughed.

D.B. watched Wendy as they walked and realized there was something different about her this morning. She wasn't guarded like yesterday, but she was tense, angry. Maybe worried. D.B. grabbed Wendy's arm and pulled her around. "Where's Eric?"

"Gone."

"Gone? Gone where? Hunting? To the bathroom?"

Wendy shrugged. "Gone."

Spock thought the two women were playing so he hopped up to them and stuck his face between them. Wendy pushed him away. "Not now, Spock."

D.B. sat down on the ground as if she'd just been struck hard in the stomach. She tried to breathe deeply through her mouth, but each breath burned her throat. Tears blinked down over her face. "He's coming back, right?"

"I don't know."

"He went after Fallows. But how'd he know where to look?"

"He took one of the prisoners."

Spock made a hand signal at Wendy. Wendy shook her head and signed back to him. "He wants to know if you have strawberry belly."

"What's that?"

"A couple years ago he got into a carton of strawberries I bought and ate them all. He was sick for two days. He thinks you have the same look he had." Wendy put her arm around D.B.'s shoulder. "Eric will be back for you."

"If he can."

Wendy nodded. "Meantime, you're welcome to stay here with me and my friends."

"I should follow Eric, try to help him."

"Suit yourself," Wendy said. She started into the Primate Center, paused, looked back at D.B. "Only you don't know where he is or how to reach him. What if he comes back for your help and you're gone, nowhere to be found?"

D.B. glanced up into Wendy's dark eyes. "You seriously think I'd fall for that bullshit?"

"Okay, part of it's bullshit. But part is true. This is the one place he could come to if he needed help. Right?"

D.B. sighed. "Right."

"Okay then." Wendy tossed the hatchet to D.B. "Make yourself useful."

D.B. used the hatchet as a cane to push herself to her feet. Her legs still felt a little wobbly. Without Eric she felt weak, deflated. Even the world around her seemed harsher, more threatening. More real. Despite Eric's own self-doubts, she knew that he was an island of sanity and humanity in a world preciously short on both. He was one man doing the right things for the right reasons.

Slowly D.B. followed Wendy into the Primate Center. Inside she found Wendy leaning over the dead body of Bolinski. She was pulling his clothes off.

"I recognize that wound," D.B. said. "Eric's crossbow."

"Yes. He killed this one and took the other as his guide. Help me with these shoes, would you?"

D.B. knelt down at Bolinski's feet and unlaced his left boot while Wendy tugged at the right.

"You slept with him last night, didn't you?" D.B. asked.

"With Bolinski?"

"Stop it."

Wendy nodded. "Yes, Eric and I made love."

"What was it like?"

"Surely you have had sex before."

"I don't mean sex. I had a lifetime of that one month." She fingered her choke collar. "From the pigs who gave me this." She pulled a sock off Bolinski's foot. "No, I mean with Eric. What was he like?"

Wendy looked surprised. "You mean you two have never slept together?"

"We sleep together every night. Only that's all we do. Sleep. He's hung up about my age."

Wendy didn't bother with undoing the buttons on Bolinski's shirt. She grabbed his lapels and tore, popping buttons all the way down the shirt front. One button landed in D.B.'s hair and Spock picked it out. Then ate it.

"That's why I ask," D.B. continued. "I know sex has got to be better than the experiences I've had."

Wendy stopped fussing with Bolinski's clothing a moment and looked over at D.B. She sat down next to Bolinski's arm and pulled her legs up to her chest. "My first time was in China. I lived in Nan-yang with my mother and her brother's family. There was a boy my age, sixteen. He repaired bicycles in his father's shop. Once he took me to the shop at night when it was closed. Right there on the work table among the greasy tools, axle nuts, derailleurs, and broken spokes, we made love. Both for the first time. He was so nervous he trembled."

"And you?"

"I thought we must be doing it wrong."

D.B. laughed. "That's what I thought my first time. Stevie Hodell in his parents' cabana at the

146

country club. They were rich." D.B. raised an eyebrow. "What about Eric?"

"Don't build it up, D.B.," Wendy said. "It was only one man, one night. Sex is not competitive. At least it shouldn't be."

"More bullshit."

"Okay. A little bullshit. It's just that it's hard to describe."

"Not when it's bad, it's not."

Wendy laughed. "You're not going to let me off the hook, are you?"

"Nope."

"Okay, it was like this: with some guys, you get the feeling during sex that having an orgasm is the whole reason they are with you. With Eric, I felt that sex was just one of the things he wanted to do with me, no more or less important than talking or eating or gardening. As if my company was the most important thing, regardless of what we were doing. And that's all the details you get." Wendy placed the sharp teeth of the hacksaw on Bolinski's arm, right below the shoulder. "Grab an arm and start cutting," she said to D.B. "We have mouths to feed."

16

Eric's wrists bled from the chafing of the handcuffs. There were ways to slip out of handcuffs, dislocating your thumb then easing the hand through. But Bao Nhu knew those methods too and had tightened the handcuffs so that Eric's wrists swelled until the hands turned plump and blue.

As they walked through the woods and fields, Eric could almost feel them getting closer to Fallows. The others seemed to tense up, walk more carefully, more like formal soldiers. Even Bao Nhu.

General Bao Nhu had been one of Vietnam's highest ranking military leaders as well as one of its most successful drug traders. He had used unknowing Vietnamese soldiers to transport the drugs through the jungle. Fallows had used the dead bodies of American soldiers being shipped back home to hide the drugs. The corpses had been cut open, plastic bags of white powder had been stuffed inside, and the bodies had been sewn up again.

Some of this came out at Fallows' trial when Eric had turned him in for the slaughter of the civilian villagers. Fallows had gone to prison. Despite Eric's testimony, General Bao Nhu's name never appeared on any transcripts of the trial.

"Quite a step down, General," Eric said. "Doing

recon work for Fallows."

Bao Nhu shrugged. "One must change with the times, Eric. I am no longer a general. After the fall of Saigon, your government relocated me to San Diego. I had a beer distributorship. Very lucrative."

"Still grabbing all the gusto you can, huh?"

Nhu smiled. "Eric, this is not personal with me. It is only business. The world changed in Vietnam and I had to adapt. Now the world has changed in California and again I have had to adapt. Fallows offers the greatest opportunities for profit."

"Just like 'Nam."

"Yes. Like Vietnam." Nhu smoothed his thin moustache with his thumb. "Don't you ever miss it, Eric? The Vietnam you knew."

"This is Vietnam," Eric said.

Nhu thought about that a moment, then laughed. "Quite right, Eric. This is Vietnam, only the faces have changed."

"Camp!" one of Nhu's men said, pointing.

On top of a slight hill overlooking the demolished city of San Diego, was Fallows' camp. Scrub brush stretched down the hill toward the freeway and city. Behind the camp stood a couple of acres of woods. From where he stood, Eric could see the familiar formation of tents, set up just as they had been fifteen years ago half a world away.

In that camp was Fallows and Tim. Finally things would be settled, one way or the other.

Suddenly Eric felt a hard kick to his kidney, the force of the blow propelling him forward to his knees. He sucked in air to keep from vomiting.

Nhu walked around in front of him. He grabbed a handful of Eric's hair and jerked his head backward. "That, my friend Eric, is to remind you that I will be watching you. Again, this is business, not personal.

In Vietnam you did what you had to and turned him in. I understand. In fact, I was able to get a new partner from the CIA and at a much more reasonable split. But now Fallows is the most powerful man around and that makes him valuable to me. Do not try anything in camp. If Fallows does not kill you, certainly I will. Understand?"

Eric nodded.

Nhu hauled Eric to his feet. "Good. Now, let's have that army reunion."

"Welcome home, Eric," Fallows smiled. The morning sun glowed behind the Halo, casting an orange tint on Fallows' white hair. It made his hair look as if it were on fire. Fallows' smile looked genuine, and in some perverse way, Eric realized that Fallows really was glad to see him. Not just to kill him, which he would undoubtedly soon do, but out of that strange affection that had made him think Eric would be a part of his activities in 'Nam.

Even stranger, for a brief moment, as quick as a camera flash, Eric was glad to see Fallows. Yes, the hate was still there, but it was for a familiar enemy, one he had reason to hate. So much of Eric's fighting lately had been with the faceless, nameless animals that attacked for no good reason. The graverobbers and cannibals and highwaymen who became mortal enemies because they wanted your shoelaces.

At least with Fallows, there was cause.

Eric appreciated the simple logic of that.

Fallows fingered the name stitched over Eric's breast pocket. "I see you found Driscol. I never thought I'd see the day Eric Ravensmith robbed graves."

"Where's Timmy?" Eric asked.

"Timmy?" Fallows looked confused. "Oh, you mean Tim. He's much too much the man now for such a baby name, Eric. Wouldn't you agree, General?"

General Bao Nhu shrugged. "This is a game between you two. I will not become involved."

Fallows' smile broadened. "The general does not appreciate what I have been doing here. Sweeping through the state, campaigning, you might say, letting people know who I am. It'll make it so much easier when I take over the place. What did Willie Shakespeare say? 'Whenever the bright sun of heaven shall shine,/His honor and the greatness of his name/Shall be, and make new nations.' "

Eric looked around the camp at the dozens of armed and grim mercenaries. " 'Men's evil manners live in brass; their virtues/We write in water.' " He stared at Fallows. "Or as the Beatles said, 'Obladee Obladah, life goes on.' "

Fallows laughed heartily, his head thrown back and his lips unsheathing long teeth. "I should have known better than to match quotes with you, Eric. Even back in 'Nam when the rest of us were stacking whores in Saigon, you were out with some ambassador's daughter talking about books. Though my spies told me you did more than talk." He winked lewdly at Eric.

"Where's Tim?"

Fallows' smile evaporated. He reached out one powerful hand and clamped it on Eric's jaw, twisting his face to the side to reveal Eric's scar. "I see you still have the little beauty mark I left you." With his free hand he pulled out his knife, the black blade glistening with oil. He laid the blade against the long white scar. "Perhaps I should remove it for you. A gesture of remorse. I could just scrape it off. Like shaving."

151

He scraped the blade against Eric's cheek until it bumped into the raised mound of scar tissue. He started slicing into it as blood seeped out from under the rubbery white line. Fallows withdrew his knife. "Manners, Eric. Watch your tone with me."

Eric said nothing. He felt the warm blood drip slowly down his cheek. A few drops clung to the scar, following it along the jaw and down the neck, disappearing into the collar of his shirt. Eric kept studying the campsite, looking for some sign of Tim. Where was he?

Fallows turned to Nhu. "What about the two men?"

"The Russians?" Eric said.

Fallows looked at Eric, surprised. "You know? Of course. How did you discover them?"

"I asked them who won the 1928 World Series and what was Lana Turner's bra size."

Fallows laughed.

Nhu interrupted. "We killed the other, the black one, as you ordered."

"Good."

"The admiral will be upset."

"Tough shit. He knew my conditions when he hired me." Fallows glanced over at Eric. "But let's not confuse my pal Eric. He's probably wondering what's going on. Or have you figured it out already?"

Eric shook his head. "I don't care, Fallows. I only came for Tim."

"All you had to do was ask, Eric me boy." Fallows cupped his hands around his mouth. "Tim. Come on out. You have a visitor."

Eric followed Fallows' eyes to one of the tents. Nothing. No movement.

"It's all right, Tim," Fallows said, grinning at Eric. "He won't hurt you. I'm here."

"Tiiimmm!" Eric shouted.

The flap of the tent opened.

Tim stepped out.

Eric was shocked at the change. His lips moved as if forming words, but no sound came out. He could only watch as this boy, only vaguely resembling his son, approached.

In size alone, Tim was different. He had grown even more than the last time Eric had seen him, standing now close to six feet. Eric had been that tall at thirteen, towering above many of his fellow students, but he hadn't grown any after that. Big Bill had played him as center on the tribal basketball team, lying that Eric was Hopi. Two years later, many of the boys Eric had stood above, now were taller than he. Six feet wasn't that tall anymore.

But it wasn't only height that distinguished Tim. Through his tight green t-shirt, Eric could see the bulge and hard lines of chiseled muscles. Tim's chest was broad, his waist narrow, his arms bunched with muscles. He looked formidable.

The worst shock was the face. Gone was the smooth child's face, quick to laughter and impish even in sleep. This was the face of a much older boy, sallow and creased with deep lines of concentration and seriousness. It was the face of someone who had not laughed in almost a year.

The hair was odd, cut short on the top, but long and straight at the back and sides, hanging down to his shoulders. The total effect made Tim look eighteen or older. Not a boyish eighteen; a tough, hard eighteen. Not interested in borrowing Dad's car or dating the cheerleader, but intent on breaking the arm of the guy who cut him off on the freeway.

Eric could see the tiny scars on his face and arms, recognized the knife cuts, cigarette burns that signatured Fallows' conditioning style. Eric's heart squeezed like a fist at his son's pain. Tears blossomed in each eye, but he fought them back. They wouldn't help.

Perhaps the most shocking sight of all to Eric, was the gun on Tim's belt. The Walther P.5 holstered within easy reach.

"Your troubles are over, Tim," Fallows said flatly. "Look who's come to save you."

Tim just stared for a moment, studying Eric as if he'd never seen him before. Then he did something that chilled Eric, that made his legs go limp and his stomach revolt in spasms of pain.

Tim smiled.

Not the smile of joy or pleasure with the wrinkles that bunched under his eyes just like Annie's smile. But the hungry, smug smile of the lizard who has cornered the beetle and wants to watch him scuttle in terror a few seconds before biting him in half.

Fallows' smile.

17

"What did you expect?" Fallows laughed. " 'Say, Wally, have you seen the Beaver?' 'Gosh no, Dad.' That sort of thing?"

Eric didn't reply. He stared at Tim, probing his son with his eyes, hoping to find that light in them that had been Tim's alone. But the eyes that stared blankly back were flat and opaque. As if a thin membrane covered them, like that of certain amphibians.

"We've been doing a little celebrating around here, Eric. Seems Tim here killed his first man last night. Oh yes, quite a fight too. Knives and booze. All that was missing was a loose woman." He winked at Tim. "That comes next, eh Tim?"

"Why are you here?" Tim said to Eric. The voice was slow and hesitant, deeper than before.

"I told you," Fallows said. "He's here to rescue you. Take you away from all this."

A few of Fallows' soldiers guffawed and snorted.

"Timmy," Eric said.

"Yes, Tim, listen to your father," Fallows said. "He wants to be your protector again, your daddy. After all, he did such a swell job the first time around. If you don't count your dead mother and sister. And you."

"This man is the man who killed them, Tim," Eric said. But he knew it was no use trying to reason. Fallows had twisted Tim's thinking through physical abuse as thoroughly as a religious cult leader. Combine that with the confusion of emotions after recently killing a man, and there was no getting through. He was still on that manic high from taking another life. Inside his mind was fighting the guilt the way the body fights a transplanted heart. He was feeling elation, disgust, and most of all, power. Eric remembered the pattern well. The first time he had killed a man, Fallows had been there too.

It wasn't in Vietnam, but in Miami Beach, just south of the city of Miami. Fallows had led the Night Shift trainees through the Everglades on a survival tour. That night they had gone into town for recreation. Private Charles Kupcek, recruited to Night Shift from a stockade for striking an officer, started picking a fight with Eric. Didn't like Indians, he'd said, poking the Hopi necklace Big Bill had made for Eric as a going-away gift. Eric didn't explain that he wasn't an Indian. He merely grabbed Kupcek's thumb and bent it back until the bigger man dropped to his knees and wailed in pain. Then he let go, said no hard feelings, and offered to shake. Kupcek stormed out of the bar. Fallows had sat at his corner table huddled with a buxom woman, never looking over at the fracas. But Eric knew he'd been watching.

That night the overpowering smell of stale beer had wakened Eric seconds before Kupcek was about to plunge a knife through Eric's chest. After a brief scuffle that awakened the others in the barracks, Kupcek lay dead on the floor, his knife planted neatly in his chest.

In the back of the barracks, Colonel Dirk Fallows sat on the edge of his bunk and smiled. Eric had the feeling that Fallows had been watching everything from the moment Kupcek had entered the barracks. Watching to see the outcome.

The way he was watching now.

"Well, Tim," Fallows prompted. "No father-son embraces? No pecks on the cheek? Hearty handshakes?"

Tim turned away and walked back to his tent, not hurrying, not emotional. Just slow deliberate steps.

"He's shy," Fallows whispered. "And modest. He cored Judd like a rotten apple. Saved me the trouble. He's become quite the team player. Not a showboat like you, Eric."

Eric looked at Fallows, controlling the hate that flowed as thick as lust. It would do no good to attack Fallows now and get killed all the quicker. As long as he was alive there was a chance for Tim, a chance to turn him around.

Fallows nodded appreciatively, as if he could read Eric's thoughts. "Smart, Eric. Very smart. Stay cool and live a little longer. You know that I can't end it all with a quick kill. Too much has happened between us for that. Still, I might indulge myself a little." He lashed out his foot, kicking Eric squarely in the crotch.

Eric doubled over, flopping in the dirt, his hands still cuffed behind him. He choked down the dizzying pain, gasped for air. He lifted his head from the dirt, caught a glimpse of Tim turning around. Tim's blank eyes took in the scene with no expression. Then he ducked into his tent.

"Children," Fallows said philosophically. "Break your hearts." Fallows snapped his fingers and two of his soldiers pulled Eric to his feet. "Well, General Nhu, perhaps it's time we shared our little scheme with our old pal Eric?"

General Nhu's voice was firm, almost angry. "I see no reason to. If you wish to kill this man, do so."

"You never really got the California spirit, General. Mellow out a little." Fallows waved for one of his men. "We're going down to see the admiral. If we aren't back in two hours, kill the boy."

"Yes, sir."

Fallows looked at Eric. "That should keep you calm."

"Mellow," Eric said.

Fallows laughed. "See, General, that's why you'll never be a real Californian. Even with all this going on, Eric still keeps his head."

The three of them started down the slope toward San Diego.

"You're going to love this," Fallows said. "The sweetest deal I've ever been in on. And if everything goes right, Tim and the general and I will be off this island in two days. Forever."

18

"That's him," Fallows said. He pointed to the lone man wearing nothing but shorts and running shoes who was jogging along the beach. Keeping pace twenty feet behind the runner were four uniformed men carrying Colt Commando assault rifles. They were barefoot. The lone runner loped gracefully across the sand, barely touching the ground before launching ahead again. The men following him ran hard and heavy, their feet chewing up the sand like a giant tractor.

"He will not like this," Nhu said.

Fallows gave Nhu a cold stare. "Who cares?"

The three of them started down the sandy slope. Unlike northern San Diego, this part of the city had not been drowned under an encroaching ocean. Instead, the land had buckled slightly, like a blanket kicked down to the bottom of the bed, lifting it a little higher out of the water.

The San Diego Bay used to separate the city from Coronado, the small island that held the U.S. Naval Air Station and the U.S. Navy Amphibious Base. But the quakes had hoisted Coronado, bumping the two land masses together. The San Diego-Coronado Bay Bridge lay in a twisted metal heap on the ground. Water still filled in the south part of the island, completely washing away Silver Strand Blvd. The city itself had been hit by a few hefty tidal waves, but most of the destruction and deaths came from the ensuing fires. The three of them had hiked along the 94 Freeway watching occasional raggedy gangs of bony people scurrying through the streets with clubs and spears and hammers. To Eric they looked like concentration camp survivors, their bodies so skinny and waxen that it was hard to tell the men from the women.

Whatever they were, they stayed away from Fallows and Nhu, who aside from handguns, also each carried new Heckler & Koch MP-5 submachine guns they'd liberated from the marine recruits who'd taken them from Marine Training Center down the street. Fallows and his men had sneaked in one night and slit the youngsters' throats. No bargaining.

The glare of the orange sun filtering through the Halo made Eric squint. Still, he could see across the beach to Coronado, the flurry of activity of men in U.S. Navy uniforms busily constructing something in the wreckage of the U.S. Naval Air Station. He could also see that the fences surrounding the base were being repaired and made thicker and higher. Outside the fence, a squad of men were carefully digging holes and planting land mines.

"They look like farmers, don't they," Fallows said of the men hunched over the mines, shoveling dirt on them.

"Not much," Eric said.

"Sure they do. Getting ready to serve up a shrapnel salad. Low calorie. Step on one of them and you'll lose weight real fast."

The three of them walked across the beach, intercepting the lone runner. The man didn't look at them although they stood directly in his path, less than twenty yards away. Eric wondered if he would just dodge around them and keep running. His men didn't seem to know, either. A couple slowed, hoisted their guns. The others kept pace, ignoring Fallows.

The runner finally looked at Fallows. An annoyed expression came over his face but he slowed to a trot and then to a stop. His appearance surprised Eric. The man was as thin as some of the scavengers they'd seen skittering through the city. Each rib strained against his pale doughy skin like a relief map. The legs were long and coltish, just bones wrapped in sinewy muscle. The fingers were so long and thin they seemed clawlike, talons of a falcon. In contrast, his head seemed too big, too handsome for the freeze-dried body. He had a wide square jaw and dark eyes that rarely blinked. He was about forty-five, Fallows' age.

"Hello, Admiral," Fallows said, smiling broadly.

The admiral didn't answer. He looked at Eric, the handcuffs. He obviously did not like what he saw.

"What is he doing here?" the admiral asked. There was no accent, but the formality of his speech indicated English as a second language.

"Admiral Jones, this is—"

Admiral Jones held up his hand. "I don't want to know who this is. What is he doing here? He is not part of our arrangement."

Fallows' smile never wavered. "Our arrangement is for me to provide protection while you and your men complete your project. Plus that other little item we discussed."

Admiral Jones looked nervously over his shoulder at his men. He leaned forward, lowering his voice. "We will discuss that later."

"Fine. I just thought you might like to know that those two men of yours that were missing didn't go

AWOL. They were killed. By this man." He nudged Eric with his gun.

Eric didn't bother denying or explaining. It wouldn't do any good.

Admiral Jones waved at his men and pointed to Eric. "Kill this man. Now."

"Whoa there, Admiral," Fallows said. "This man is my prisoner."

"He killed my men."

"He's killed some of mine too. Look at this uniform he's wearing. Used to belong to Driscol, one of my best men. He will be killed, I promise. I'll do it myself."

Admiral Jones looked skeptically at Fallows. "I am beginning to worry about you, Colonel. I hope I didn't make a mistake about you."

"You hired me to protect your men. That's what I've done."

"I'm beginning to wonder if I really need you after all."

Fallows shrugged. "Well, of course that's up to you. I offer a service, but this is still America. You don't have to avail yourself of it." Fallows' smile became thin and wolfish, his voice slick but threatening. "Who knows how many gangs of roaming banditos might see what you're up to over there and start sneaking up on you at night, cutting throats and such. Could put your whole project in jeopardy. Not everybody here is as mellow as my men and I."

Admiral Jones pondered the implied threat while his men anxiously fingered their guns. Eric watched Fallows and Nhu, who held their guns casually, almost as if they forgot they were even carrying them. If it came to a fight though, Eric knew the Russians would be all be dead within three seconds. Chances are, however, Eric would also be dead.

162

"I've got to whiz," Eric said.

The admiral looked confused. "What?"

"Piss," Fallows explained. "Don't they keep you up to date on your American slang when they send you on these missions? Christ, they go through all this trouble of dressing you up like Americans, giving you American names and phony ID right down to letters from girlfriends in Kansas and such, and you guys don't even know what a whiz is."

Eric nodded at the admiral's Nike running shorts and shoes. "I see by your outfit that you are a runner."

The admiral, embarrassed by his not knowing the slang, was happy to change the subject. "Marathoner," he said proudly. "You?"

"Twice. A few half-marathons. Not so much anymore." Eric turned his handcuffed wrists to Fallows. "I still gotta go."

Fallows stared at Eric, then grinned. He fished the key from his pocket and unlocked the cuffs. "You wouldn't be stupid enough to try anything, would you, Eric?"

"I just want to take a leak." He gently massaged his wrists, the skin hanging in shredded flaps, bleeding. He turned his back to the group of men and walked a few paces away. He unzipped his fly. Eric heard the sound of the safety of Fallows' SMG clicking off.

"I know my men searched you, Eric. But just in case, when your hand comes out of your fly, it better have nothing in it but your dick."

Eric shrugged. "Don't worry. It's not lethal."

From behind him they could see the yellow stream of urine splashing into the sand.

"You see, Admiral," Eric said over his shoulder as he continued to piss. "You'd be making a big mistake underestimating Colonel Fallows here. The man is a pig with no morality whatsoever."

"Ah, a testimonial," Fallows said.

"Something about what I'm doing makes me think of you," Eric said. Then to the admiral. "So, even though he's obviously blackmailing you and you think you can be rid of him right now because your men outnumber him, don't. He knows what he's doing." And suddenly Eric shifted around and let his stream of piss hit another spot in the sand, washing over a small clump of weeds.

"*Vidish!*" one of the admiral's men said in Russian, pointing. They stared at the clump of weeds.

Slowly the urine hosed away the sand and a face began to appear underneath. The eyes were squeezed closed and there was a hollow reed in the man's mouth that had been hidden among the clump of weeds. Piss splattered across the man's face.

He jumped to his feet, revealing the shallow hole he'd been lying in and the three lines of sand that had covered his body so no one could see him. Or the H&K MP-5 SMG he carried.

Eric was zipping his fly again by the time the rest of Fallows' men were unearthing themselves and leaping to their feet. Each armed. Each aiming their weapon at the admiral. There were six of them.

Fallows was laughing, the sound harsh and metallic. "You still have it, Eric." He faced Admiral Jones. "Like Eric said, Admiral, I know what I'm doing. If I'd wanted you dead, they'd be sifting sand for your remains right now. But I need you and you need me, so let's cut the bullshit and get down to business. Twenty-four carat business."

The admiral wiped the sweat from his forehead with the back of his hand while he looked from Fallows to Eric to Nhu to the six armed and sandy men. He crooked a finger at one of his one men and the soldier produced a clean yellow t-shirt. The admiral pulled it on. Immediately it soaked up wet spots of sweat. On the chest was a large blue insignia, a sort of modified checkmark. Over that the word Nike.

"Okay," he said. "We will discuss this matter. But not in front of him." He nodded at Eric. "Either kill him now or we discuss nothing."

Fallows looked at Eric. "What can I tell you, Eric? The guy thinks he's Joe Stalin."

"Tell him you can't kill me, you need a fourth for bridge."

"You heard him, Admiral," Fallows said. "But I'll tell you what, I'll send him back to camp. Nhu, you'll take him, won't you?"

Nhu's dark face was as emotionless as carved hickory. "I think I should be here during negotiations."

"I can talk for both of us, General," Fallows insisted. "Don't you trust me?"

Nhu smiled slightly. "I have done business with you before, Colonel."

"Dickens," Fallows said. The man Eric had pissed on stepped forward. "Take Eric back to camp."

Dickens, his face splotched with the gritty mixture of sand and urine, glared at Eric. "Alive, sir?"

"Relatively," Fallows answered. He tossed the handcuffs to Dickens. "You'll need these."

Dickens patted his SMG. "No I won't."

"Yes, you will."

Dickens yanked Eric's arms behind his back and snapped the cuffs on tighter than they'd been before. Dickens booted Eric in the back, sending him to his knees.

"Don't kill him," Fallows said.

"I won't," Dickens said.

"I was talking to Eric."

Dickens looked a little frightened as he hauled Eric to his feet and pushed him ahead. He stuck his SMG in Eric's back and nudged him forward toward the camp.

Fallows waited until Eric and Dickens were out of sight. He nodded at two of his men. "Follow them, but stay out of sight. If he tries anything, shoot off his legs."

General Nhu watched the two men run off. He shook his head at Fallows. "I would feel better if Eric were dead."

"Tonight," Fallows grinned.

19

Eric ran his tongue over his swollen lip. The blood had crusted some. Dickens had hit him there. The tender knob on his shin still ached where Dickens had kicked him with those steel-tipped boots. A deep pain smoldered high on Eric's right thigh. Dickens had tried to kick him in the crotch, but Eric had managed to turn and catch the blow on his thigh, though he moaned and doubled over as if Dickens' kick had been accurate.

Eric had looked up from the ground, blood dribbling down his chin, and said firmly, "That makes us even."

A fearful look crossed Dickens' face again and he backed away. Then he remembered the gun in his hands, the fact that Eric was handcuffed, and he stepped boldly forward. "You picked the wrong man to piss on, chump." He hauled back and kicked Eric solidly in the ribs. "It's not so funny now, is it?"

Eric had to admit it wasn't. Especially now that they were back in camp and Eric had the time to inventory his wounds. The kick to the ribs had cracked something because he could feel the rattle in his chest whenever he took a deep breath. He stopped taking deep breaths.

He was alone in Fallows' tent. Dickens had shoved him to the ground, tied his ankles until the circulation was cut off, and then pounded some tent spikes through his shirt and pants, pinning him to the ground like Gulliver in Lilliputia.

Dickens had grinned down at him. "Now we're even."

The only part of his body Eric was able to move was his head. He shook it sadly. "Now I owe you."

"You're just lucky I don't gotta piss, man, or you'd be drinking it right now. Tell you what, though. I'm gonna go out and drink me some beer and see what happens. By then you should be real thirsty and won't mind if it's a little used."

That was half an hour ago. Eric could hear Dickens drinking with several other men. Eric could have killed him on the way back, there had been half a dozen opportunities that wouldn't have required much effort. But he'd spotted the two-man tag team that Fallows had sent behind them. He could imagine their orders. Maim but don't kill.

He'd wait for a better time.

Unfortunately, this was the better time. No one around to watch him work his clever miracles. Problem was, he was fresh out of miracles. He was lying on top of his handcuffed hands, his feet were bound, his clothes were staked to the ground so he couldn't budge. Outside the tent a man was loading up on beer so he could come in here and piss on Eric. And soon Fallows would be coming back, no doubt to kill him. The quick kill wouldn't suit Fallows' purposes. He would have to turn it into a show, a major Broadway production with music and a chorus. He

168

would stage it as religious entertainment, a voodoo ritual where his men could see that Fallows could defeat any enemy. Eric had once read of a high school football coach who used to bite off the head of a toad before every game to get his players motivated. Tonight, Eric was going to be the toad.

He struggled against the stakes, not worrying about what he would do if he managed to pull them free. One thing at a time. Big Bill Tenderwolf once had Eric tie him up, hands and feet, as tight and escapeproof as Eric could manage. Eric was only seventeen at the time and learning different sailing knots from a book his father had bought him. He trussed Big Bill up like a spool of cable, tying nautical and Hopi knots, and a few he made up on the spot. By the time he was finished, he had a Blackwall hitch, bowline, cat's-paw, clove hitch, fisherman's bend, sheet bend, square knot, surgeon's knot, and a dancing snake. Big Bill had rolled round the floor of his house, writhing and flexing, struggling, his face turning red with exertion. Eric had sauntered smugly into the kitchen, brought a six-pack of Big Bill's favorite beer back, pulled the ring, and loudly sipped, smacking his lips.

"Great stuff, Bill," Eric had said.

"Okay, Eric," Big Bill had said, lying like a beached whale in the middle of his colorful Hopi rug. "Untie me."

"No way, pard. You told me you could be out of anything I tied within half an hour. It's barely been ten minutes."

"I was wrong. Come on, untie me."

Eric took another swig of beer. Big Bill watched, licking his lips.

Eric shook his head. "You told me not to untie you no matter what you said. Made me promise."

Big Bill struggled some more, twisting and turning on the floor like a worm on a griddle.

Eric drummed his hand on top of the beer can and sang, "Writhe and roll is here to stay, it will never die."

Finally exhausted, Big Bill had stopped struggling and just lay there. "Okay you win. How much more time?"

Eric checked his watch. "Ten minutes."

"Give me a sip of beer while I wait it out."

Eric grinned broadly as he knelt next to Big Bill. "You owe me a new bow. That was the bet, a new bow or I weed your garden for a month."

"That was the bet. Now give me some beer."

Eric lifted Big Bill's shaggy head with one hand and put the can to his lips with the other.

Suddenly Big Bill's huge hands were free of the rope and around Eric's neck. Within seconds Big Bill had Eric on the floor, wrapped in the Hopi rug, and the rope tied tightly around the rug. "We call this pig in the blanket."

"Shit! How'd you escape?"

Big Bill grinned, sipped beer. "There is no such thing as true escape. One can only change captors."

"That doesn't make any sense," Eric had said, twisting inside the rug.

"Maybe not. But it'll give you something to think about while you're weeding my garden."

Lying on the floor of Fallows' tent, Eric smiled at that memory. "Writhe and roll is here to stay," he repeated, wincing at how much like D.B. he'd sounded. Maybe Big Bill had been right. Eric had

170

been captured by graverobbers, a woman and her ape, and then a Vietnamese general. But it was Fallows that had captured him long ago, the day he'd killed Annie and Jennifer and kidnapped Tim. Ever since it was as if Eric had been hooked on a long fishing line and even though he thought he was attacking, it was Fallows who was reeling Eric in. He'd been a captive all this time and hadn't known it.

No more!

Eric concentrated on one stake at a time. The one next to his shoulder. The metal stake hammered through his sleeve, the cool aluminum scraping against his skin. He shrugged his shoulder, heaving up with his whole body. The effort brought him back down on his cuffed wrists with a thump, crushing his fingers.

He tried again. He bucked up, rolling away from the stake. It loosened. He repeated the movement several times, each time the stake shifting in the dirt, rocking slightly, then wiggling, and finally, with one mighty heave, it pulled free.

He did the same with his other shoulder, but this time the shirt tore before the stake moved. Eric kept pulling until the patch of shirt staked to the ground tore completely loose of the rest of the sleeve.

"Who wants to come with me?" he heard Dickens shout outside the tent.

Eric froze.

"Come on, you can watch me piss in his face."

Someone else laughed. "One more beer and we can *all* piss in his face."

"Yeah," a few others chorused.

"Okay," Dickens said amiably. "One more. But I get to go first."

Eric kicked up with his legs, trying to jerk free the stakes in his pants cuff. Sweat soaked his face and clothes as he listened to the men outside hoisting their drinks. It wouldn't take them long to finish.

He heard a noise behind him and sat up.

"Father."

Eric turned, saw Tim crawling under the tent. Tim stood up and stared at his father. Eric could see the confused emotions struggling in Tim's eyes. He had a man's body, a man's experiences, but he was still a thirteen-year old boy trying to sort the emotions. Eric had to be careful.

"Visiting hours?" Eric said.

Tim pressed his lips together until they drained white. He kicked at the stakes in Eric's pants until Eric easily uprooted them. Eric waited for Tim's next move. Tim seemed just as unsure as to what it would be. Then with a deep breath, he unsheathed the knife at his belt and stooped at Eric's feet. He looked into Eric's eyes, but Eric could see little that was familiar in them.

"You must promise first," Tim said. "You will leave and never come back."

"I'm taking you with me," Eric said.

"No. I belong here. We are survivors. We take what we want because we are strong. You wouldn't understand."

"Come with me. Explain it to me then."

Tim hesitated. Eric could see the longing in his son's eyes. Tim shook his head violently. "No. We aren't the same anymore. I used to think I wanted to be just like you. Good, fair, compassionate. What good did that do the people you loved, the ones who trusted you? Mom? Jenny? Me? Your way didn't protect us."

Each word from Tim was worse than the steel-toed kicks from Dickens. Eric tried to harden himself to them, reminding himself that they were more Fallows' words than Tim's. "Cut me loose, Tim."

"Do you promise?"

"Yes."

"You'll go and not ever come back?"

"I promise."

Tim quickly sawed through the ropes that bound Eric's feet.

Eric felt the blood swimming back into the numb ankles. "Do you have a key for these?" Eric leaned forward to reveal the cuffs.

"No, but I think I can handle them." He grabbed a pair of aviator sunglasses from Fallows' bunk, twisted the wire rim, and picked at the lock. In less than a minute he had opened the cuffs.

"Nifty trick," Eric said, jumping to his feet. "Where'd you learn it?"

"Fallows," Tim said. "He's taught me a lot."

Eric nodded. He peeked out the tent flap and saw Dickens draining the last of his metal cup of beer.

"I go first," Dickens said, thumping his chest.

"We'll go watch."

"No way. I don't want you perverts grabbing for my cock when you see how big it is." He laughed and marched toward the tent.

Eric backed away, putting his finger to his lips. Tim nodded. Eric held out his hand for Tim's knife. Tim handed it to him.

"Thirsty, maggot?" Dickens said as he swaggered into the tent.

Eric slapped his hand over Dickens' mouth and

173

dragged him the rest of the way into the tent.

"Need any help finding it?" one of the men shouted. The others laughed.

Eric stood behind Dickens, holding his mouth closed. He could smell the beer and fear in Dickens' sweat. Eric plunged the knife straight into Dickens' stomach, then pulled the knife quickly upward as if unzipping a jacket. Dickens' hands went to his stomach as he tried to keep his guts from spilling, but it was like holding the groceries in a torn bag. Eric released him and he fell to the ground in a slushy heap.

Eric looked over at Tim, but there was no expression in his son's eyes. The boy stood calmly and held out his hand for his knife. Eric gave it to him. Tim pointed toward the back of the tent. "Go. I've left your crossbow and quiver outside the camp in the woods."

"Come on," Eric said to him.

"No."

Eric took a step toward him and Tim pointed his knife at his father.

"You promised," Tim said.

Eric nodded. He started toward the back of the tent. Suddenly he whirled around, brushed aside Tim's hand with the knife, and punched his son in the neck. Tim's eyes rolled up as his knees buckled. Eric caught him as he fell, swooped him up in his arms. He grabbed a gun and Tim's knife and slit open the back of the tent, and carried Tim into the nearby woods.

"You may be full of shit, Dickens," one of the men yelled, "but ain't nobody that full of piss. Here we come."

174

Eric found the crossbow leaning against a tree. He slung Tim over one shoulder and the crossbow and quiver over the other. Then he ran as fast as he could, the hard metal bow bouncing on one shoulder, the soft unconscious boy bouncing on the other.

And behind them, the angry shouting of men tracking him.

20

"You lied," Tim said.

"I've done worse."

"Is that supposed to impress me?"

Eric shook his head. "It's supposed to sadden you."

They sat in the back seat of a burned out Volvo in Balboa Park. The park was 1,158 acres that once had been a cultural and recreational center bordering San Diego's business district. They could see some of the exhibit halls along El Prado that had been built in 1915–16 for the Panama-California International Exposition. Fallows' men had lost them a couple of miles back and would be returning to camp to tell the colonel. The San Diego Zoo was less than a mile away at the northern end of the park. But the blow to Tim's neck had put him out longer than Eric had thought and he'd stopped to bring him around. He seemed okay now.

"Fallows would have hurt you for helping me escape," Eric explained.

"You've made things worse."

"I saved you from him."

Tim's face scowled in anger. "He saved me from you. People like you. Sure, he would have punished me, it's what I deserved. But then it would have been

176

over. Now you've compromised me. When he catches me again, he'll have to start the whole torture process over again. You've tainted me. He can't be sure what you've done to my mind."

"What I've done? For God's sake, Tim, he's brainwashed you, programmed you away from me, from you, from who you are."

Tim shrugged. "Who's to say? He's just swapped your program for his. How do I know which is right for me until I've tried both?"

Eric looked out the smashed window of the Volvo. A battered koala doll lay near the car. One of its eyes was missing. It reminded him of Deena and her band of graverobbers.

"Let's go," he said.

"Yeah, right. You've got no argument, so it's 'let's go' because you say so. Right?"

Eric looked over at his son, the dark brooding eyes. Taken out of context, it was almost a typical father-teenage son exchange. They might have been talking about the length and color of his hair or his slipping grades. And like most such exchanges, Tim was right. There was no logic that could be explained or understood. It was just might makes right. Eric was bigger, had Tim's knife and gun. Every action he made was reenforcing Fallows' teachings. The strong should dominate the weak because they can.

"We'll talk later," Eric said, but that sounded lame even to him.

They climbed out of the car and Tim immediately tried to run. Eric grabbed his arm and yanked him to a stop. "Can't you give me the same chance you gave Fallows?"

"You had me for twelve years. It got me a dead mother, sister, and kidnapped. He's had me for nine months and I'm part of the most powerful group in the world."

"This island isn't the world."

"Sure it is. For us. Besides . . ." He stopped.

"What?"

"Nothing."

Eric looked at him, remembering Fallows' bragging that he could get Tim off the island. "Besides, he can get you out of California and I can't. Right?"

"Yes."

"With the Soviets?"

"Yes."

"How? What's going on?"

"What's the difference?"

Eric tightened his grip on Tim's arm. "Tell me, Tim."

Tim looked at Eric's hand on his arm and grinned wryly. "The Russians have come in in a submarine. Somehow they slipped past the blockade outside."

"Why? What are they doing here?"

"Building a small missile base. One missile is run completely by remote control."

Eric thought for a moment, then nodded. "Yes. They're coming in disguised as U.S. Navy, erecting a missile that will no doubt also have U.S. markings. That way if it's ever discovered by the outside world, or the people who saw them ever questioned, it will look as if the U.S. used the opportunity to exploit its own people. The adverse publicity will be worth it. If not, they have one more warhead close to the U.S."

"The colonel heard about them while we were travelling," Tim said. "He came down here and told them he'd keep the locals off their backs and not hassle them in exchange for some ammunitions and equipment. The Russians didn't have much time, so they figured it was worth it and agreed."

"Wisely," Eric said. "What about the gold?"

"That's a private deal with the admiral. Fallows offered to buy fare for Nhu, himself, and me. For gold. Lots of gold."

"And our Admiral Jones, in true capitalist fashion, decided what the motherland didn't know wouldn't hurt it. And he and his crew would be richer for the experience."

"Something like that."

Eric pulled Tim after him. He was moving quickly now, anxious to get under cover.

"He'll be coming for me," Tim said.

"I know."

"Where will you hide?"

Eric caught the 'you.' Tim was telling him that they were not together, reminding him that Fallows would kill Eric, but not Tim. Where to hide? Eric considered heading east, lose them in the desert. He could go north, hide out in the forests and mountains while he deprogrammed Tim.

But even as he considered each option he knew there was only one place he could go. The zoo. Because even if he didn't go there, Fallows would assume that he had, and he would swoop down on the place and kill D.B. and Wendy. The time it would take to do that could give Eric enough of a headstart. Enough for him and his son to escape. But as Big Bill had said, there was no true escape. Only different captors. And to leave D.B. and Wendy to Fallows would put Eric back on Fallows' fishline again.

He headed toward the zoo, dragging Tim behind him.

"With Fallows," Tim said, "I have a chance to get off this island. Isn't that what you'd want for me?"

Eric said nothing, kept walking.

"If you loved me like you say, wouldn't you want to give me that chance? I gave you your chance back in the tent."

Eric had no answer. Maybe Tim was right. Perhaps love did mean giving Tim to Fallows if it meant getting him back to the rest of the world. Maybe back there Tim could see what a mutant someone like Fallows was.

But Eric didn't want to take that chance. If Tim couldn't learn that lesson here, then he'd never learn it. In a few hours he would have his chance, because that's how long Eric figured before Fallows and his men reached the zoo.

21

Eric straddled the barbed wire atop the zoo wall. He draped his shirt over the wire where he stood so Tim could step over it. Eric need not have been so cautious. The gangly, slightly clumsy child he remembered was now long-legged and agile. Tim stood on the narrow ledge of the wall with perfect balance and no fear.

The transition had been just as sudden for Eric when he had been Tim's age. Like Tim, Eric at twelve had excelled at the more cerebral pursuits: crossword puzzles, chess, drawing. On the playground or while visiting the Hopis with his father, Eric's play with the other children had always made him feel inept. Balls did not naturally take to his hands, no matter the shape or goal. Throwing, kicking, dribbling, all were equally mysterious.

Then at thirteen, a sudden growth spurt shot him up and then his body could whip around the other children with such ease he had to laugh. Balls became allies. They flew like trained falcons wherever he sent them. It was as if the first twelve years his body had been tied, bound tight like the feet of young Chinese girls. Then suddenly the ropes had been cut and there wasn't any physical challenge he couldn't master.

Eric watched Tim stand with easy grace on the narrow wall and remembered the little boy who had come home from school crying because he was always the last one chosen for kickball. Eric had hugged him, told him his body was resting, like in a cocoon, giving him a chance to develop his brain. That the other kids who were already athletic, might always rely on their bodies and never get the chance to train their minds. This was Timmy's "brain time." The rest would come later, he promised. Timmy accepted his father's word and took to books and chemistry sets and piano and writing poetry. School tests placed him in the genius percentile. Teachers and counselors suggested special schools for the gifted. Eric and Annie had refused. They kept Timmy in public school among his friends and tutored him themselves, allowing him to flourish in any direction he wanted.

They had tried to be the best parents possible. Now as Eric looked at Tim's tall frame, black marble eyes, he wondered if maybe Tim wasn't right after all. Perhaps Eric had let him down, screwed up royally. Made the kind of mistakes every parent swears they won't make. Maybe he babied him, or didn't baby him. Gave him too much or too little love. Surely the lessons he'd spent twelve years teaching his son couldn't be so easily replaced. Not if Eric had done his job properly.

A huge rock pelted the wall near Eric's feet, bounced off and fell into the brush at the foot of the wall.

"Halt! Who goes there?" D.B. said, stepping out

from behind a tree. Her makeshift slingshot dangled from her hand. "I heard that line in some old war movie. How's it sound?"

"Like an old war movie," Eric said, hopping down from the wall. Tim jumped next to him, landing with such grace that Eric couldn't help feeling a little pride in front of D.B. Silly, he knew, but the feeling was there anyway. They'd been apart so long. He wanted to take Tim in his arms and hold him tight, hug him the way he used to after those bad playground experiences. No good. The look in Tim's eyes forbade any contact yet. Eric was pained that the only physical contact they'd had since their reunion was Eric knocking him out and carrying him away. Not unlike the way Fallows had taken him in the first place. Eric could find water in a hundred miles of desert; find food in five feet of snow. But could he find his son in the boy/man standing next to him now?

"Tim?" D.B. asked, obviously surprised by his appearance.

"Tim, this is D.B." Eric said. "A friend."

Tim looked at D.B., but gave no acknowledgement. Then to Eric, said, "What kind of friend?"

"A friend," D.B. said. "As in 'You've Got a Friend.' You know, 'You just call out my name.' That sort."

"James Taylor," Tim said.

"Carol King wrote it."

Eric listened to them, thinking how much they sounded like Tim and his sister, Jenny. The two of them bantering, arguing, complaining about each other until their voices sometimes formed a background music around the house. "Yuppie Muzak,"

Annie had called it.

"Where's Wendy?" Eric asked.

"Back at the lab doing her mad scientist routine."

Eric started jogging toward the lab, Tim and D.B. in tow. "We haven't much time. Hurry."

D.B. snorted. "I heard that line in the same war movie." As they ran, she reached out and pulled Tim closer to her. "Stay on this path, Tim. There are crawly slimy things with teeth and nails."

"I'm not scared."

"I am. That's why I want you close."

Tim stayed close to D.B. as they ran.

How easily she did that, Eric marvelled. The most convincing argument *he'd* given the boy was a right cross to the neck.

The sun had faded out behind the Halo. There were no more sunsets or sunrises. Just a leaking away of light followed by a sort of darkness that wasn't quite black, more like a gray fuzziness. It was getting that way now.

Eric pointed to the bruise on D.B.'s forearm. "Racquetball?"

"Elephant. Named Dizzy. Whacked me with his trunk while Wendy was checking his teeth. Had a cavity the size of a golf ball."

In the lab they found Wendy writing. When she looked up Eric could see the relief on her face, though she immediately forced it off.

"I told you he'd be back," D.B. said.

"Like a bad penny," Wendy joked. She stood up and Eric wanted to hug her but he felt uncomfortable with Tim watching.

"Tim, this is Dr. Chen."

"Wendy," she said, offering her hand.

184

Tim shook. "Another friend?" he said archly. "Like in the song?"

"Pardon?" Wendy said.

"Never mind," Eric said. "We have only a few hours, so let me give you your options now."

"Options?" Wendy asked. "What are you talking about?"

"Time. We don't have much of it. Fallows and his men will be here soon. That gives us only two options: stay and fight or run and hide."

Wendy bristled. "I'm not leaving. This is my work, my life. If I leave, every animal in this zoo will be butchered and eaten within days. Or they'll kill each other."

"If you stay," Eric said, "Fallows will butcher you."

"This is a big zoo, Eric. There are many dangerous animals loose. Many places to hide."

"Not from the colonel," Tim said, with a slight smile.

Eric felt the challenge in Tim's voice. Stay and fight Fallows, prove who is stronger. Eric was tempted to accept, not just because of Tim, but because such hatred as he felt needed to be exorcized. Nevertheless, this was not a symbolic battle between good and evil for a matinee crowd. It was their lives. "My advice is to leave. Let them have the zoo. You'll be alive."

"I've seen death before. I'm not afraid."

"Jeez," D.B. said. "You're not afraid, the kid's not afraid, Doc Rock's not afraid. Am I the only one around here who's scared of these creeps? I say we grab Spock and take off."

"Spock?" Tim said.

"Yeah, Spock. Cutest gorilla you'll ever chat with.

You'll see."

Eric shook his head. "We can't take Spock. Just the four of us."

"Oh shit. A moral dilemma. I was hoping to make it through without one."

"What's the problem?" Tim said to his father. "If they want to stay, let them. You don't have to."

Wendy looked at Tim, then at Eric. "He's right, Eric. You found what you came for. There's no reason to stay."

Eric knew she wasn't playing the martyr. He could see the compassion in her eyes. She saw that Tim was not as Eric had described him, saw the agony Eric felt for his son's condition.

"D.B.?" he asked.

"Christ, you don't give a girl much time for moral dilemmas. I'm not too good at this."

"Why don't you just clobber them and haul them away like you did me?" Tim said.

D.B. spun toward him. "Why don't you quit sassing your dad or I'll clobber you myself." She looked at Eric. "If we stay, what are our chances?"

"There are things we can do. Precautions. Traps. Warning systems. It's not hopeless."

"You really know how to whip up troop morale," D.B. laughed. "Anyway, let's give it a shot. I always wondered what Davy Crockett felt like at the Alamo."

"Dead," Tim said.

"We're going to have to free the animals," Eric said.

"No." Wendy shook her head adamantly. "They'll

186

end up killing each other. Or these friends of yours will shoot them."

"No choice. We'll need the diversion to move around. How much more barbed wire do you have?"

Wendy didn't answer. She glared at Eric.

"Look, Dr. Chen. Twenty trained and armed men are about to come pouring into your little paradise here. All we've got are one crossbow, one slingshot, Tim's Walther, and the two SMGs you brought back. Unless you want to get blown out of Eden a second time, we're going to need to balance things out. Now where's the goddamn barbed wire?"

"Hidden. In the snake exhibit."

"Nice touch. Got a map of this place?"

"I do," D.B. said. She pulled a folded paper from her pocket, brushed off the lint. The paper was dirty from the rocks she carried in her pocket for her slingshot. "I found a bunch of these over at the ticket booths."

Eric unfolded the leaflet. It described the guided bus tour and the Skyfari Aerial Tram, the Children's Zoo, where to rent wheelchairs and buy film. In the middle was a crude map where all the exhibits were. "Pencil?"

Wendy unclipped a pen from her pocket and handed it to him.

"Here and here," he said, drawing lines on the map. "That's where we'll build the fences. Nothing fancy. Just enough wire to keep the animals where we want them."

"They'll be able to break them down in a few hours," Wendy said.

"A few hours is all we'll need."

"I don't get it," D.B. said.

187

"Two Knights' Defense," Tim said.

"Yeah, sure. That explains it."

Tim looked at Eric as he explained to D.B. His expression revealed nothing. "It's a chess opening analyzed by Greco in 1630, then explored further by the Berlin master Von Bilguer in his *Handbuch*."

D.B. slapped her hip. "Works for me. Let's do it."

Tim looked at her. Eric noted it was the same frustrated look he used to give his sister when she teased him during his pompous moments. "To simplify," he said sarcastically, "he intends to create an opening for the colonel and his men to enter, but by releasing the deadlier animals and fencing them just so, he's forcing men and beasts alike to move in the same direction in the same cage. It's like a giant maze with lots of dead ends. Right?"

Eric nodded. "While they're busy looking for animals, we'll be able to pick them off. Even up the odds."

"What do you want us to do?" Wendy said.

"You've got a generator, haven't you?"

"Christ, how do you know?"

"Some of the medicine you'd have needed to inoculate these animals requires refrigeration. I saw the refrigerator was removed from the lab." He pointed at the scratches on the floor. "That's where it used to be."

"We moved that the first week. Figured it was best if no one knew we had a generator or fuel."

"Where?"

"The Reptile House. I figured if anybody sneaked in here for food, reptiles would be the last place they'd go."

"Good thinking. I'll use the generator to rig some

kind of early warning device, maybe hook into the P.A. system. I'll need your help for that."

"What about us?" D.B. asked.

"You two will string the wire where I've drawn the lines on the map. Neatness doesn't count. Just get it up in a hurry."

"You want *me* to help?" Tim asked.

"Some reason you can't?" Eric said.

Tim stared at him for a minute.

D.B. grabbed Tim's arm. "Good, now that that's settled, let's get to work. Anybody know any good songs for stringing barbed wire?"

"What's that noise?" D.B. asked.

"Ssshhh." Tim put down the barbed wire and walked forward with his wire cutters.

Spock saw the wire cutters and bounced happily toward Tim, reaching for them.

"Keep him quiet," Tim said. His eyes searched the darkness.

"He likes tools," she whispered. "Likes to lick them like popsicles."

"Ssshhh." Tim stalked a few feet from where they'd been stringing wire. Something was out there.

D.B. held onto one of Spock's arms to keep him still, but he chuckled and dragged her along. "God-damn it, Spock, knock it off."

Suddenly, out of the brush a wolfish looking animal sprang over the wire. It landed on the concrete pathway. One of its back legs was bleeding where it had been raked on the barbed wire.

Tim pointed his gun at the animal.

"No, don't shoot," D.B. said. "It's a Chinese

dhole."

"A what?"

"Kind of a dog. A wild dog from China. Wendy explained about him. He's okay, just scared like the rest of us." She grinned at Tim. "Well, maybe not all of us."

Tim gave her a stern look, which softened into a smile. "Maybe a little scared. You don't see many Chinese dogs around. He's pretty."

"Yeah, his coat is almost golden."

Spock ran toward the Chinese dhole and the animal turned and sped off, Spock loping lazily after it for a few feet, then bored, returning to D.B..

"Hand me the wire cutters," D.B. said, unfurling a roll of wire.

Tim tossed the cutters to her.

"Tell me about your sister," D.B. said, snipping through the metal.

"You're not her."

"Were you this bratty with her?"

Tim shrugged. "I don't remember. I mean, I remember us arguing about stuff a lot. But I also remember her sticking up for me to Mom and Dad. Taking me to the movies. Making popcorn for the TV movies on Saturday nights when Mom and Dad went out. She always burned the popcorn. I couldn't understand how she could always burn the popcorn." He stared at the strands of barbed wire in his hands. "How hard is it to make popcorn anyway?"

"I don't know. I always used those prepackaged pans that puff up like a nuclear power plant."

Tim went back to work, not speaking.

"Give him a chance, Tim," D.B. said solemnly. "You don't know how much you've meant to him these past months. You're all he's thought about."

Tim smirked at her. "Not the only thing."

D.B. threw the wire cutters on the ground. "Watch your mouth, kid. I wish what you're thinking were true. Believe me, I tried to make it true. But your dad's got funny notions. Maybe I don't always agree with them, but I respect them. One funny notion he's got that I'm not so sure about is that you're worth all this trouble."

"I didn't want to come here. I was happy with Colonel Fallows. At least with him I don't have any hopes or expectations. He says you want something, you take it."

"Quite the philosopher, huh?"

"It works."

"Yeah, I know. I've seen it work." She tugged on the choke collar around her neck. She turned back to her work. "Let's finish this up, okay?"

They went back to work in silence. Spock wandered off exploring, but occasionally came bounding back and pestering D.B. until she stopped and tickled him for a minute. Then he'd wander away again.

D.B. snipped through another strand of wire, stood straight, and shook the cutters at Tim. "And another thing, Timothy Ravensmith. I know how being a prisoner can scramble your brains some. I was one until your daddy busted me loose. And at first I was just as mean and snotty toward him as you are. I don't know why I was, except I felt tired of being owned, that all I'd done was exchange masters. But I was wrong. Just took me a while to figure that out."

"You don't understand," Tim said. "What are we supposed to do now? Live here with you, the Chinese

191

doctor, and your ape. Ozzie and Harriet Go Native. Father Knows Beast. Or are we going to run? Keep moving, knowing all the time that Fallows, with more men and better weapons, is bound to catch us. In the meantime we live on scraps and hide. At least with Fallows you don't hide from anyone. They hide from you. Why not go with him now and save the trouble?"

D.B. shrugged, turned back to her work. "I don't have an answer. If that's what you want, do it."

"You mean go? Right now?"

"Sure."

"And you wouldn't try to stop me?"

"Would it do any good? You're bigger and stronger."

Tim hunched over the bale of barbed wire looking confused. The usually smooth skin of his forehead was knotted with concentration. D.B. watched him out of the corners of her eyes. Maybe he knew that she was lying, that the moment he tried to walk away she would grab her slingshot and pelt his legs until he couldn't walk. She owed Eric that much. But maybe he believed her.

After a few minutes of silence, Tim walked over to her, stood next to her, tapping the wire cutters in his hand.

D.B. looked up. "What?"

Tim smiled. "Can I help you?"

D.B. sighed with relief and smiled back. "Sure. Jump in here."

Eric stripped the two wires and twisted them together. He jumped down from the wall. "That should do it."

"Do what?" Wendy asked.

"Anyone touches the wire on this section of the wall, it turns on your cassette player and pumps the music through the P.A. system."

"The wall around here is big. What if they don't pick this section?"

"They will. It's the second easiest. I've made sure of that."

Wendy shook her head. "I may not be a Warlord, but why would they come through the second easiest location when they could come through the easiest."

"Because Fallows will suspect a trap there. At least I've made it look like a trap."

She smiled at him. "It must be tiring being so devious."

"Exhausting. A Warlord's work is never done." He looked at his watch. "Speaking of which, it's time to free the animals."

"This is the hardest part." She looked up at him. "It's like killing them."

Eric took her hand, felt the callouses on her palms. He was going to explain the need again, but he saw in her eyes that she already understood everything he would have said. She was just expressing her sadness, not asking him to do anything about it. That made him feel helpless. "Let's do it," he said, leading her off.

They walked carefully through the zoo, aware that some of the dangerous animals were already loose. To the wild animals there was no Fallows or Ravensmith, good or evil. Just food. Good and evil tasted the same to a South African cheetah.

"This way," Wendy said, pulling Eric down a path.

"Even loose in the zoo, the animals are territorial. I pretty much know where they all are and where they stay. It's just a matter of rounding them up one at a time and getting the hell out before another one comes in for the kill."

"Sounds simple enough."

She laughed. "So simple that when this is all over and if we're still alive, you're going to help me recapture each and every one."

They began releasing the animals where the fences were already complete. In some cases it was just a matter of putting a board across a moat for the animal to walk over. The giraffes, because they're top-heavy, are trapped by a 30″-deep ditch around their exhibit. They're afraid to step down. A couple planks and the three of them were soon stomping along the perimeter wall like guards on patrol.

"They aren't vicious," Wendy said.

"I know, but they'll be just one other thing Fallows' men will have to look out for."

Releasing several of the other animals took greater care. A couple of lions were particularly cranky and Wendy and Eric dashed off the moment the cats started across the makeshift bridge.

On their way to the next animal, Eric almost stepped on a fleeing duck. It was tiny, with slick brown feathers and white comet markings around the eyes.

"Mandarin duck," Wendy said, running beside him. "In Japan and China it's a symbol for marital fidelity."

"We've got a similar symbol over here. The shotgun."

Wendy laughed. "I never realized how much fun it

was preparing to die."

"On the fun scale, it ranks slightly below bowling and above miniature golf."

They released a couple Siberian tigers, rhinos, water buffalos, four Sumatran orangutans, and even a giant Galapagos tortoise.

"We'd better check on Tim and D.B.," Eric said. "We can't release any more animals until their fences are finished."

When they got there, they weren't prepared for what they saw.

D.B. lay on the ground, dazed. Blood trickled from the corner of her mouth.

Tim was gone.

Eric quickly unslung the crossbow from his shoulder. "Fallows," he said, cocking the bow. "He's here."

22

"No," D.B. said. Her voice was weak and hollow, as if piped up from some distant well.

Wendy knelt beside her, gently lifting D.B.'s head. D.B. tried to sit up the rest of the way. "Don't," Wendy said. "There may be internal injuries."

"Internal injuries, my ass," D.B. said. She struggled up, caught her breath. Her eyes were clearer, her voice stronger. "A right cross, that's all it was."

Eric grabbed her under the arm and pulled her to her feet. "Which way did they take Tim?"

"They didn't," D.B. said, looking down. "Tim hit me and ran off."

Eric stared at her. "Tim?"

"I don't understand it. We were talking, laughing. He was telling me about some dog he used to own, how big and fluffy it was, how it reminded him of Spock—"

"Tim never had a dog," Eric said. "His sister was allergic."

"Why that little jerk. He was playing me along the whole time. Damn!"

"Something else he learned from Fallows," Eric said grimly. "The power of the disarming smile, the charming conversation."

D.B. brushed the dirt from her pants. "He learned

196

well. He had me going. Sorry, Eric."

At that moment Spock trotted out of the brush and onto the path toward them. He ran up to Wendy and signed for a tickle.

D.B. smiled. "At least Spock has his priorities straight."

"Now what?" Wendy asked Eric.

"Now I go after him. Try to stop him before he escapes or gets attacked by one of the animals we set loose."

"I know the zoo better," Wendy said. "Better let me go with you."

"I'm going too," D.B. said. "The brat stole my slingshot."

Eric took a key from his pocket. "Let's go to the aviary and get the guns."

At the aviary, they found another surprise. The lock had been picked and Tim's Walther was gone.

D.B. picked up one of the SMGs. "At least he left these. That's a good sign. I think the Tim you first brought here would have taken them all just because he could."

Eric handed Wendy the other SMG. "We'll split up, try to find him before he gets out or Fallows gets in."

Wendy checked the gun with an expert's eye. She snapped out the retractable buttstock and fitted it to her shoulder. She caught Eric and D.B.'s surprised expressions and explained, "Even a child in Vietnam knew how to handle a gun. Perhaps especially a child."

D.B. checked the curved magazine.

"It holds thirty rounds," Eric said. "Minus whatever they may have used before I took them."

"What do you want us to do when we find Tim?" D.B. asked. "I mean, he's pretty determined to leave."

"Stop him," Eric said.

"You mean shoot him in the leg or something?"'

Eric remembered his last rescue attempt of Tim. Fallows shooting Tim in the leg to keep him from escaping. "Yes," Eric said. "If you have to."

Each went in an opposite direction toward the wall. They planned to move in a counterclockwise sweep. But they were barely out of each other's sight when the p.a. system switched on and Ike and Tina Turner started singing "Proud Mary."

"Fallows!" Eric said.

"Left a good job in the city . . ." Tina Turner said.

23

"I should have known," Fallows laughed. He grabbed the electrical wires Eric had attached to the barbed wire and yanked them loose. Ike and Tina Turner stopped singing.

Fallows jumped down from the wall and stared out into the darkness. "Very tricky, Eric."

A twang echoed, followed by a loud tearing sound, like someone ripping a page out of a phone book. Then a thud. Fallows looked up and saw one of his men grasping the arrow in his chest as he dove off the wall and bellyflopped in the dirt next to Fallows' feet. Fallows crouched down. "Down! Everybody down!"

Twelve of his men were already over the wall. Another five were still climbing. The rest he had left back at camp. One of his men, Greene, ran up and squatted next to Fallows.

"Where to, Colonel?" Greene asked.

"Get down!" Fallows told him.

"Yes, sir, I just —"

Another twang and ripping sound. Greene flopped face down, the point of the bolt sticking out of his back.

"Move out," Fallows said. "Garvey, take six or seven men and go that way, along the wall. Essex, take the others and go the opposite direction. When you meet, go straight through the middle."

"Yes, sir," Essex said.

"What about you, Colonel?" Garvey asked.

"I'll do some tracking on my own."

Essex and Garvey called some names and took off in the directions they were ordered.

Fallows waited.

Eric watched Fallows. He could just make out the bristly white hair above the rock. Not enough to take a shot at. Fallows had always had white hair, at least as long as Eric had known him. Even as a young man of thirty. It peaked over his forehead into a V, giving him that hungry look. It wasn't gray, but pure white, the absolute absence of color. Just as his brain had the absolute absence of conscience.

Eric glanced around, saw Fallows' men sneaking off along the walls. Eric didn't have a clear shot at them, nor did he have enough arrows to just keep taking pot shots. It had been his intention to split them up and he'd succeeded at that with only two arrows.

Now he had to find Tim.

There was a movement over by the drinking fountain. Eric hefted his crossbow. A small orangutan poked the water button. Nothing happened. It made a screeching sound and wandered off. A huge tortoise lumbered into view, walking with such slow and deliberate steps it looked as if it were hauling two tons of coal in its shell.

Fallows still had not moved. Thin tendrils of white smoke curled up from behind the rock. The bastard was smoking a cigar. He knew Eric was waiting for him, and with his men searching the grounds, he knew he could afford to wait.

But Eric couldn't. He had to find Tim before he climbed the wall or was captured by Fallows' troops. Tim wouldn't have tried either the openings that Eric had made knowing Eric would be around those two sites. And he knew where the inside wires were being strung to keep the animals so he would avoid them. That really left only a couple of places for him to try to jump the wall. Eric hesitated. Fallows was still there, armed, sure, but here, within his grasp. They could finish it between them right here, right now.

Eric stood up. With a quick glance at Fallows' white hair feathered above the rock, Eric ran off looking for Tim.

"Manusco," Essex said. "Quit dropping back. You're supposed to be scouting ahead."

"Fucking snakes everywhere, man," Manusco said. "I don't mind scouting, but I hear noises up there I ain't never heard before. Like some goddamn Tarzan movie."

"Just get your ass up there or I'll shoot it off. That's Tarzan for you."

Manusco cursed and jogged up ahead. He didn't see why they couldn't walk the concrete trails just like he'd done when he'd visited this place years ago. He and a couple of Marine buddies had come down from the El Toro base. They'd picked up a couple high school girls in front of the ape grotto and left with them. Turned out one was only sixteen. Manusco took her. Never did get to see the rest of the zoo.

He looked over his shoulder. In the dark he couldn't see Essex or the others anymore, but he could hear them rustling behind him. Then he heard some rustling in front of him and snapped his gun to his shoulder. He didn't see anything. There it was again, but it wasn't in front of him at all. It was above him. He looked up.

A striped Siberian tiger dropped out of the tree, front paws pushing into Manusco's chest. Manusco's gun went flying into the brush. It didn't matter. The tiger's claws batted Manusco's face, ripping his face away with one clean swipe, like erasing a blackboard. Manusco screamed and the other soldiers answered with a burst of gunfire that scared the cat away.

"Save your goddamn bullets!" Essex yelled. "At least until you see what you're shooting at."

They came upon Manusco writhing blindly on the ground, his face raw meat.

"Help me, Essex," he pleaded.

"No can do, buddy," Essex said. "Colonel wants me to keep going." Essex stooped over and picked up Manusco's SMG. "We'll try to pick you up on the way out."

"For God's sake, Essex! I can't see."

"Let's go," Essex waved to his men. They walked away. Fifty yards later, Westmeyer pulled Essex aside.

"Christ, man, you could've at least finished him off."

Essex shrugged off Westmeyer's hand. "We may need the bullet."

"Spock?" D.B. whispered.

The ape lumbered over to her, sitting at her feet. He signed to be tickled.

"Not now," she said. There hadn't been time to lock him up. Fallows had come sooner than they'd expected. And she certainly didn't have time to nursemaid a gorilla.

She stalked along the wall, the SMG gripped

tightly in her hands. Her palms were so sweaty she was afraid that if she pulled the trigger, the gun would jump out of her hands.

Spock grunted crossly at her, signing again for tickles. D.B. pushed him away. Or at least she pushed his chest. He didn't budge.

Then she heard the growling of a large cat, a lion or tiger, and the screams of a man. The burst of automatic fire. At the sound, Spock jumped back and dashed off in the opposite direction.

D.B. saw a flash of yellow fur running through the brush as the Siberian tiger took off past her. She heard men's voices and walked toward them.

They weren't making much effort to be quiet. They didn't have to. Half a dozen men with sub-machine guns could make as much noise as they wanted.

She crouched down under a bush, waiting for them to march past her. This is always where the big fat snake comes slithering up, she thought, looking around. But there were no snakes or spiders. Just a small douc langur, its monkey face bristling with white whiskers. Wendy had pointed one out earlier, explaining that they were endangered because they came from such war-ravaged areas as Vietnam, Laos, and Cambodia. And now San Diego, D.B. thought.

When the men were well gone, D.B. hopped up and continued searching for Tim. She had walked less than twenty yards when a hand whipped around her mouth. She could taste the salt and dirt of his skin.

"Whoa," he said, squeezing her so hard, the air whooshed out of her chest. She went limp, though she was still conscious. His hand still clamped over her mouth, he turned her around so she could see him.

She had never seen him before. But she knew right

away from the arrogant smirk, the dark eyes, the white hair, who he was.

He pulled his knife out and poked the point against her belly. She tried to pull back but he held her fast.

"Tim," he said. "Where's Eric hiding Tim?"

D.B. knew from looking into his face that he would stab her. She could refuse to answer, the kind of heroic gesture she imagined Faye Dunaway or Vanessa Redgrave might make. But she was neither; she wanted to live so badly she started to sob uncontrollably. Mucus snorted from her nose and she didn't have the strength to wipe it away.

"Where?" Fallows demanded, his grip tighter, the knife now piercing a quarter inch of skin.

She closed her eyes, for a moment envisioned Eric leaping from a tree, his crossbow firing in mid-air, the arrow slicing through Fallows' neck. But when she opened her eyes, Fallows was still there, his cruel grin hovering inches away from her face. His breath was strangely sweet, like birch bark.

Then the loud crashing of branches, the whooping noise, the thundering gallop of heavy steps. D.B. looked over Fallows' shoulder expecting to see elephants or rhinos stampeding. But what she saw was one lone gorilla named Spock charging at Fallows.

Fallows pushed her away and drew his Walther out.

Spock was less than ten feet away. And coming.

D.B. scrambled for her fallen SMG.

Dr. Wendy Chen felt a certain exhilaration crouched in the brush behind a refreshment stand waiting for the voices to come closer. These were American soldiers coming, perhaps among them the very one who had killed her father. Not likely, she knew, but it helped her prepare for what she knew she must do.

She did not blame all Americans. She didn't even blame soldiers. She blamed people who liked war, who enjoyed fighting. Eric was not such a man, she could tell, though she could also tell he was good at it. These men coming were such men. Killers by choice.

She waited as they walked closer. Eric had warned them not to engage the soldiers as a group, to only pick off the strays, and only when they could hit and run away. She hoped there would be one stray. She lifted her gun in anticipation.

"What the fuck's that?" one of the men said. She could barely see their outline in the dark.

"A giraffe, idiot," someone answered.

Gunfire chattered loudly. Wendy watched the giraffe wobble on its long legs, then topple over into a tree.

"Now it's just a rug," the first man said.

"Don't waste bullets, Collins."

"I just don't like big animals following us around."

"It wasn't following us, Collins, it was eating from the top of that tree."

"Well, fuck him anyway."

They walked on.

"Ouch. There's barbed wire all over the place, man."

"And that giraffe is blocking the path."

"Thanks, Collins. Now we've got to walk over that thing."

Wendy watched them climb over the carcass of Nina, the Masai giraffe who'd been bred and raised right here in the zoo. Their boots mashed her delicate ribcage. One man sliced a swatch of her spotted fur for a souvenir.

Wendy didn't think about it. She just pulled the trigger. The SMG shook in her hand, the muzzle flashing as bullet after bullet cut through the brush. Two of the men fell over dead. The others dove for cover and returned fire.

Wendy darted to the left, but a bullet chopped into her calf, dumping her on the ground. She scrambled on hands and knees, but another bullet skimmed off her back and dropped her face-down in the dirt. She tried to crawl, but the pain was too great.

"Collins, you and DeVito check it out. See if we got him. The rest of you, keep hunting for that kid."

Wendy heard them whooshing through the brush as they came toward her. She picked up her gun and rolled onto her side for a better shot. But when she tried to hook her finger around the trigger, she discovered the trigger wasn't there. Bullets had clipped off the trigger and busted up the firing mechanism. The gun was useless.

"Over there!" Collins said.

She heard them both running now. She closed her eyes, just for a moment, she thought. When she opened them again, they were standing next to her. Collins was nudging her wound with his foot.

"Looks bad, honey," he said. He looked at his partner. "You believe this, DeVito. Fucking woman, and a slant at that."

DeVito raised his gun. "Let's do her and get back."

"Not so fast," Collins said. "She's not too bad looking. A quick hump before we do it couldn't hurt anything. You can have sloppy seconds."

DeVito thought about it a second, then shook his head. "Fallows would have our asses." He aimed his gun again at Wendy's chest.

The arrow entered DeVito's face just below the right eye. It spun him around as if in a clumsy square dance. His finger flexed against the trigger and he fired a dozen rounds into the ground as he fell.

Collins opened fire randomly, spraying a cluster of trees. The arrow that got him couldn't be heard over his gunfire. Nevertheless, it punched through his heart with a satisfying thump that knocked him on his back. He managed to flop about a few seconds before dying.

Eric rushed to Wendy's side. "How bad?"

"Falls somewhere between bowling and miniature golf."

He smiled, examined her back. "Not bad."

"You wouldn't lie to me, would you?"

"Yes. But this time I don't have to. Just stay put." He dragged her to a tree and propped her up against the trunk. He handed her Collins' gun. "Try not to break this one."

"Eric?"

"What?"

"I got two of them."

"Plus these two, that leaves two or three in their party. Have you seen Tim?"

She shook her head. The effort spent a spasm of pain through her back. She clenched her teeth.

Eric ran off, disappearing so silently into woods that she wasn't even sure when it happened. One moment she was watching him running, the next he wasn't there.

By the time Eric caught up with Garvey, it was too late.

Garvey's men had rejoined with Essex's group. And Essex had Tim.

"Quit squirming, kid," Essex said. "You're safe now. We got ya."

"Where'd you find him?" Garvey asked.

"Going over the wall back there. Got his leg tangled up in the barbed wire."

"Thanks, guys," Tim said. "I was looking for you."

"Then why didn't you call us?" Garvey asked. "We were all over the place."

Tim rubbed his scratched leg. "Couldn't take the chance. If Ravensmith heard me he'd be all over me. In fact, he could be out there right now, taking aim on us."

Garvey and Essex looked around. Their men quickly crouched down, bringing their weapons up.

Eric continued to watch. There were too many of them now. Any attack could get Tim accidentally killed.

"We'd better get back to the colonel," Essex suggested.

They formed a circle around Tim and double-timed it back along the wall.

Eric followed along, keeping hidden in the brush. The animals wouldn't attack them now. Too many.

When they arrived back at the place where they'd climbed in, General Bao Nhu was waiting with a few other men. They must have scaled the wall after Fallows' men split up.

"Where's the colonel," Nhu asked.

Essex shrugged. "We left him here."

"Maybe we should send out a patrol," Garvey said.

"You volunteering, Garvey?" Essex grinned.

"Are you?"

"I've had enough of this place. Fucking animals everywhere. I don't even like vegetables, let alone all this shit."

"I'll go look for him," Tim offered. "I know my way around."

Eric moved closer. He couldn't tell if Tim's offer

was a ploy to escape them, or if he was really concerned for Fallows. Either way, once he was out of their sight, Eric could try to grab him again.

"I think not, Tim," Nhu said. "We will wait three more minutes, then leave. Colonel Fallows is quite capable of taking care of himself."

"Another testimonial, General," Fallows said, stepping out of the brush. A smear of blood spread across his forehead. He limped slightly. He put his hand on Tim's shoulder. "And you, thanks for offering to look for me."

Eric raised his eyebrows. The distance would be tricky, but possible.

But Fallows pulled Tim in front of him, slapping the boy fraternally on the back. Now Tim was positioned between Eric's arrow and Fallows. Fallows glanced out into the woods while he spoke to the others, as if he knew Eric was there taking aim.

"Let's get out of here," Fallows said. "Last one in, General, is last one out. You and Essex keep us covered."

Nhu stiffed at Fallows' insulting orders, but he turned and aimed his gun in Eric's general direction. Essex did the same.

"Ready? Now!"

As Fallows and Tim climbed the wall, Essex and Nhu sprayed bullets randomly around them.

Eric heard a few chew the leaves next to him and he ducked lower, unable to get off a shot. The shooting and climbing continued as Fallows men scaled the wall under the cover of Nhu and Essex's arc of bullets. Eric was frustrated, anxious to at least return fire, but any movement now could be fatal.

Finally only Nhu and Essex were left. Nhu pulled rank and started up the wall. Essex opened fire.

With only one of them shooting, Eric waited for

his chance, popped up, and fired a bolt into Essex's chest. Nhu was hanging from his hands on the edge of the wall, pulling himself up. When he looked over his shoulder and saw Essex collapse, he scrambled up the wall.

Eric ran forward a few more yards, dropped to one knee, cocked and loaded the bow, aimed, and fired. The bolt zipped through the night and pinned Nhu's left shoulder to the wall. Nhu's left hand immediately lost grip of the wall and he dangled from one hand. One of Fallows' soldiers who was in the process of gingerly stepping over the barbed wire, turned, saw Nhu, and opened fire on Eric's running body.

Eric dove behind an exotic tree as the soldier's bullets battered the tree trunk into flying chips. Eric loaded his bow, rolled over to the other side of the tree, and sent an arrow fast as a bird blink into the man's stomach. The soldier fell over, his leg tangled in barbed wire. He flopped hard against the wall, dangling there by one twisted leg.

Nhu couldn't climb or hold on any more. His hand started to open and he dropped to the ground. His weight pulled the bolt from the wall, but a bloody splotch still dotted where it had carved a hole.

Eric waited to see if anyone would come back for Nhu. He wasn't surprised that no one did.

After a few minutes, he walked over to the former general. Nhu had broken the bolt and pulled the point the rest of the way through his shoulder. He was packing patches of cloth he'd torn from his shirt against the wound when Eric arrived. Eric bent over and picked up Nhu's SMG that lay less than ten feet from him.

"No point in going for it, was there, Eric?"

"Not much."

"You would have only put another arrow in my

other shoulder, am I right?"

Eric shrugged. "Or leg. I hadn't decided."

"The point is, you want something from me or you would have killed me on the first shot. Correct?" The general winced from pain as he pressed his bandage to his wound.

Eric looked around. Where was D.B.? Now that the shooting was over, she should be coming out, talking away or singing some appropriate snatch of lyric. "D.B.?" he shouted.

No response.

Just the clattering of animals, screeching of birds. No D.B.

He resisted the temptation to run and look for her. If she was dead there was nothing he could do. If she was hiding out of earshot, she'd come out sooner or later. But right now he had General Bao Nhu and he needed information.

"Fallows was in a hurry to leave," Eric said. "That's not like him, especially knowing I was here."

Nhu coughed, grasped his chest. "I think the fall hurt me more than your arrow."

"Are you going to give me trouble?" Eric said.

"Me? Eric, you know me better than that. I know that sooner or later every man talks. It is simply a matter of finding out not only how much pain he will endure, but what kind of pain. Some men can take physical pain for days—whippings, beatings, broken bones—but take this same man and threaten to cut off his nose, or balls, and he will talk immediately. Each man is different, yet in the end we are all the same. We surrender. Me, I've decided to cut out the middle man. What do you want to know?"

"Why Fallows left."

"Admiral Jones, whose real name by the way is Buddenov, gave him only six hours to be prepared to leave on the submarine. Naturally his men knew nothing of our plans. Well, his plans now. Doesn't look like I'll be making the departure, does it?"

"No."

He sighed. "I thought not. I imagine you'll try to stop Fallows from departing with your son."

"Why is the sub leaving now?"

"They have finished their little base. It was nothing all that complicated. The hard part was keeping the local scavengers away who would have swarmed down from the hills with their rakes and spears and killed the Russians and tried to steal the submarine, even though none could operate it. These are troubled times, Eric."

"So they're waiting for the right time to sneak through the barricade outside."

"Very good, Eric. Yes, there will be some distraction outside that will pull the ships out of formation, a burning trawler or something, and Admiral Jones and his American clones will slip through unnoticed. With Fallows and Tim aboard. However, if Fallows is not there at departure time with the gold, he does not go."

"Once the sub is gone, what's to prevent us from going in and destroying the missile?"

"They've installed an explosive very similar to a neutron bomb. If the base is tampered with, the whole thing goes up and the radiation will kill everyone around for miles. But it leaves the buildings standing, therefore the U.S. will get the blame. After all, as far as anyone investigating could tell, it's a U.S. missile base."

Eric thought that over. "Naturally, the bomb is harmless until the security system is activated."

"Naturally. They wouldn't want any accidents blowing it too soon."

"And they wouldn't activate it until their sub was out of range of the bomb's effects. They'll wait until they're underwater and have cleared the Halo."

Nhu nodded. "They expect the conventional mine field will keep the curious away until then."

"How much time is left?" Eric said, pointing his bow at Nhu.

Nhu looked at his watch. "Two hours and sixteen minutes. After that the sub will be gone and so will Fallows and your son."

Eric stared at Nhu. Nhu's discussion of torture was not merely philosophical. It was the result of years of practical experience. Eric had even heard that in recent years Nhu had freelanced to certain South American countries, teaching them the intricacies of torture, offering demonstrations on political prisoners.

"What now, Eric?" Nhu asked.

Eric grabbed him by the back of the collar and dragged him away from the wall.

"What are you doing?" Nhu pleaded, fear starting to tinge his voice.

Eric leaned him against a tree.

Nhu held up his hand. "Eric, I can tell you more. Where the gold is. If you beat Fallows to it, you could buy your way home. You and your son off this horrible island."

Eric jammed the crossbow up against Nhu's good shoulder and pulled the trigger. The bolt punched through the shoulder, nailing Nhu to the tree. He screamed in pain.

"I'm cutting out the middle man," Eric said.

Nhu tried to pull the bolt out of his shoulder, but his free hand was too weak from the wound in that shoulder. He couldn't even dislodge the arrow from the tree. He slumped. "Why this foolishness, Eric?"

"I pay for information. I'm giving you a chance. You get free and climb the wall, you live. If you make it, I wouldn't advise going to Fallows to warn him. I only pay once."

Eric ran off in search of D.B.

When he found her, he cried out, *"No!"* and ran faster than he had ever run before.

24

D.B.'s body was sprawled half in a bush. Eric could see drops of blood on the tiny green leaves, as perfectly round and wet as globes of dew.

"D.B.," he said, carefully easing her out of the brush. He laid her out on the ground. Blood soaked the side of her neck. Her hair on one side of her head was sticky and matted with blood. He pulled the hair away from her face and saw that part of her ear was gone. He lifted her head onto his knee. Her eyes fluttered, opened.

"Shit, that hurts." Her voice was crusty, as if she were using it for the first time after sleeping for a hundred years. "I guess I'm alive, huh?"

"Looks it."

She laughed, coughed, then sang weakly. " 'Uh, uh, uh, stayin' alive.' Better than the Bee Gees, right?"

Eric tore a piece of cloth from his shirt, spit on the end, and dabbed it against the wound in her neck. "Looks like a bullet put some skid marks on your neck."

"Yeah, that hurts. But my damn ear. The lobe feels like it's on fire."

"It's not," Eric said. "Those are phantom pains."

"Phantom my ass. The pain is real."

"I don't mean it doesn't hurt. Just that your lobe doesn't hurt. It's not there. Another bullet."

"My ear's gone?" she croaked. "My goddamn ear's gone!"

"Just the lobe." He smiled.

D.B. closed her eyes. Eric could feel her body quake with silent sobs as she fought for control. He was impressed with how quickly she won. She opened her eyes. "Guess I can always get my good ear pierced again. Won't break up a pair of earrings that way." She started to get up.

"Hey, don't rush it."

"You kidding? Now that I've lost part of my ear, all I gotta do is lose an eye and you'll go nuts for me."

Eric laughed as he helped her to her feet.

"Where is everybody?" she asked.

"Wendy's wounded, nothing too serious. Fallows and the others have taken off."

"Tim?"

"They got him."

She looked around. "Where's Spock?"

"I haven't seen him."

"What do you mean? He was charging out of the woods like some furry Lone Ranger. That bastard Fallows had hold of me. He tried to shoot me, but Spock was on him just as he was pulling the trigger. Saved my life."

"I saw Fallows leave."

D.B.'s eyes went wide with fear. "God, no!" She ran off. Eric followed her.

They saw him at the same time, both running toward him, Eric's longer legs getting him there first.

"Oh, please, no!" D.B. wailed.

Spock's eyes were open, but he was dead. There were three bloody holes in his chest and one in his

216

arm. Eric could tell from the trampled brush what had happened. Fallows had fired at Spock, wounding him, but Spock had given chase. But once Fallows put enough space between them, he turned and finished the gorilla off with a burst to the chest.

Eric looked at D.B., who knelt next to Spock stroking the fur on his forehead.

"I'm not going to cry, if that's what you're expecting," she said stiffly. Blood webbed across her cheek and neck as intricately as warpaint. "I just want to get Fallows."

"Let's get you and Wendy mended first." Eric was conscious of how little time he had to catch Tim and Fallows before the submarine took off. He grabbed D.B. by the arm and led her back to Wendy.

Wendy had already done a good job of first aid on herself, and even managed to drag her body around until she found a branch to use as a cane.

Eric and D.B. helped her to the infirmary while Eric explained what General Nhu had told him.

"We'd better get going then," D.B. said, adjusting the bandages on her neck and ear.

Eric didn't have time to argue with D.B. It wouldn't have done any good. He could see the hate in her eyes, in her whole body. It was a tightness that couldn't be relaxed until she had confronted Fallows. Eric understood.

"You'll be okay?" Eric asked Wendy.

"Sure. To tell you the truth, I probably wouldn't go with you even if I could. This zoo is my world. I've got a lot to do getting them back to their own exhibits before they kill each other. I've got to tell Madonna about Spock. Sounds silly, but they understand about death. She's going to take it hard." Her dark Oriental eyes prismed with tears. She flipped her long hair back over her shoulder, using the same

217

gesture to secretly wipe her eyes.

On their way back to the wall, they saw something moving near the tree where Eric had left General Nhu. It ducked into the bushes and kept running.

"He's loose," D.B. said, readying her gun.

"Wait," Eric told her. He ran closer. The general was still there. Or at least part of him was. His torso had been chewed almost in two. A leg was gone.

"Jesus," D.B. said, coming up behind Eric. "What did that?"

Eric picked up a rock and threw it into the brush. A giant lizard skittered away, a half-chewed leg still in his mouth. "Komodo Dragon Monitor," Eric said.

"Ugly mother," D.B. said.

They scaled the wall quickly and jogged at a good clip toward Coronado, where the submarine was based. They could see a few fires flickering across Balboa Park, but they avoided them.

"How are we going to destroy the missile base?" D.B. asked as they ran.

"Who said anything about that? I just want to get Tim back."

"But the missile threatens the U.S."

"Let the U.S. worry about it. They can drop leaflets on it. It's my son I want."

D.B. didn't say anything to that. She ran in silence next to him until they stood on the ridge overlooking the beach that led to the submarine. They could see the small white shack that housed the missile, the barbed wire around it, the big billboard-sized sign with a battery-run light shining on it. It read: U.S. Navy Installation. Stay Out. Danger. Active Mine Field.

On the beach, Fallows and Tim walked among eight of Fallows' soldiers. They headed toward the submarine.

Eric and D.B. dropped to the ground to watch.

Fallows waved for his men to fan ahead of him and Tim. Three of the men had flashlights to lead the way. Fallows reached out and held Tim back. Unaware, the rest of the men continued to march ahead.

"What's he doing?" D.B. asked.

Suddenly Fallows unslung his submachine gun and opened fire on the backs of his men. All eight fell to the sand, the dropped flashlights shooting crossing beams of light across the sand. Fallows went to each man and pumped an extra bullet in his head. He tossed the empty magazine and slapped in a fresh one from the body of one of his men.

"What'd he do that for?" D.B. asked.

"He's getting ready to complete his deal with the Soviet admiral. He doesn't want his own men around asking where he's going and why he's not taking them with him. The rest of his men are probably back at camp waiting for him."

Fallows had hold of Tim's wrist and was running through the navy base. On the other side of the base, Eric could see the submarine waiting.

"What do we do now, Doc Rock?"

Eric stood up. "We improvise."

Eric picked up an SMG from one of the dead bodies. D.B. grabbed a couple extra clips for hers. She tagged after Eric, barely keeping within twenty yards of him.

Eric's first stop was the missile base. He climbed the roof of one of the buildings near the missile shack. From here he could see Admiral Jones and three sailors standing on the deck of the submarine waiting for Fallows to arrive. The admiral checked his watch constantly, tapping it with his fingernail.

His three sailors stood in their American uniforms waiting. The submarine itself was an American Fast-Attack type, used mostly for detection. He could see the name *Mississippi* on the side of the sub. Right down to the last detail, he thought.

He could see Fallows and Tim still running through the maze of buildings and trailers toward where the submarine was waiting. Another few minutes and they would be aboard, on their way to the outside world. Tim lost forever.

Eric turned, aimed his SMG at the mine field. He fired a string of bullets that stitched through the mine field in a zig-zag pattern. Finally one hit a mine and a muffled explosion sounded. He fired again, eventually hitting another. The mine exploded, throwing waves of sand in all directions.

Admiral Jones looked up, startled.

Eric took aim. They were too far out of range for him to actually hit one of the men. But he ought to at least be able to hit the damn ship. That's all it would take. He opened fire. The first few rounds fell short, kicking up sand. The next burst plunked into the water near the ship. The third burst pinged into the sub and sent the admiral and his men scurrying for the hatch. Within seconds, the submarine was airtight and moving away.

Eric fired a few more rounds to keep them going. He stopped and looked over at Fallows. Fallows pointed a flashlight in Eric's direction, but the distance merely diffused the light, swallowing it before it could reach Eric. Then the flashlight clicked off and Fallows and Tim were gone.

Eric slid down the roof and climbed back to the ground. D.B. was waiting for him.

"What's going on?"

"The sub's gone. Fallows is coming this way."

She hefted her gun. "Good."

"Not good. Last time he shot at you he had a 400-lb. gorilla charging him. This time he won't miss. There's something else I want you to do, and there's no time to argue."

"What, go home and cook a good meal?"

"Go over to that shack and cook a good missile. You wanted to destroy the thing for God and country and Betsy Ross. Well, you've got to do it before that sub goes under the Halo. After that, any tampering with it sets off the neutron bomb."

D.B. smiled excitedly. "Finally a job worthy of my talents." The smile dropped from her face. "What'll I do?"

"Burn the place down. The fire should melt some of the circuits before they can transmit the signal."

"How do I get through the mine field?"

"You don't. You've got to make some Molotov cocktails or something. They used a few of the jeeps while they were here. There must be some gas in them you could siphon. You've got about ten minutes. Go!"

D.B. hesitated, kissed him quickly on the lips, and ran off.

Eric didn't really think much of her chances of actually destroying the equipment, but the task would keep her out of the way. Whatever happened next was between Eric and Fallows. And Tim.

Fallows unlocked the trailer door and pulled Tim inside. The twenty-foot trailer had been used as a construction headquarters while a new recreation facility was being built. The blueprints on the drawing board indicated they were going to call it the "Catalina Canteena." It would have ping-pong tables, pool tables, and twelve lanes of bowling.

Against the back wall of the trailer was a beat-up old GE refrigerator. Fallows kicked through the rubble on the floor, dragging Tim behind him. When he got to the refrigerator he yanked open the door. Inside, the shelves were stacked with boxes of gold. Jewelry, teeth, watches.

"Looks like your dad did it to you again, Tim," Fallows said. "He screwed up your chances of getting off this island for good." He slammed the door shut and the whole refrigerator shook. "Now all we've got is this fucking gold. Not worth anything. I've killed most of my men. We'll have to start all over again." Fallows brushed his hand over his buzz-cut white hair. He smiled, revealing back teeth as white as his hair. "It shouldn't be hard to recruit people. Soon we'll have an even bigger and badder army. Right?"

Tim nodded.

"Let's get out of here." Fallows led Tim back out the trailer, stopping to grab a set of keys he'd nailed to the bottom of the drafting table. "One important lesson is to always have an escape plan. I've got a jeep outside filled with gasoline I bought from one of the Russian sailors. Even sailors like a little gold now and then."

"What about my dad? He's out there."

"On foot. We'll be out of here in seconds. By the time he hunts us down again, he'll be facing fifty armed men." Fallows kept a firm grip on Tim's wrist as they walked outside. A jeep stood with the hood open and wiring strewn everywhere as if it had been hit by a grenade.

Fallows pushed Tim into the passenger's seat while he climbed behind the wheel and inserted the key.

"This thing will never start. Someone must have gotten to the wires," Tim said.

Fallows turned the key and the engine kicked in perfectly. "Those wires are just camouflage. I stuck them there myself. They aren't connected to anything. There are all kinds of tricks you haven't learned yet. But you will. In time."

Fallows shifted into gear and the jeep pulled out. "Colonel!"

The voice boomed at them and Fallows hit the brakes. Ahead, standing on the roof of the trailer they had just come out of, stood Eric Ravensmith. His clothes were shredded, his face was streaked with dirt, but his eyes were steady. His crossbow was cocked, but resting on his hip, pointing skyward. In the hazy darkness of the Halo, he looked like some nightmare figure.

Fallows grabbed Tim and pulled him in front of him as a shield. He punched the gas pedal to the floor and steered the jeep as he drew his Walther from his holster.

Eric knelt, aimed, and fired his bolt. The stubby arrow drilled through the jeep's windshield, shattering the glass and stabbing into the seat next to Fallows. It barely grazed his arm, but the glass flying into his face made him lose control of the jeep. His foot still flooring the gas pedal, he drove the jeep straight into the trailer.

The impact tipped the trailer over, throwing Eric to the ground. His crossbow flipped out of his hands during his fall and dropped on the other side of the barbed wire fence surrounding the base.

The jeep turned over, dumping Fallows and Tim onto the ground. Fallows recovered quickly, the wound on his leg aching again where that ape had clobbered him. Tim was dazed and Fallows quickly dragged him to the trailer, propped him against the underside, and handcuffed the boy to the axle.

Fallows wiped the blood from the gash in his forehead where windshield glass had cut him. He still held his Walther. "Come on, Eric. Let's finish it."

Eric shook his head again but the haziness wouldn't clear. His sight was a little fuzzy, as if he were staring through gauze pads. He looked around for his crossbow, saw it lying on the other side of the hurricane fence topped with barbed wire.

"This is what you wanted, isn't it?" Fallows said from the other side of the trailer. "Showdown at high noon?"

Eric smelled gas. A gunshot blasted, followed by a muffled whoosh and Eric could see the smoke streaming upward. Flames peeked over the edge of the trailer.

"Uh oh," Fallows said. "We've got a problem here, Eric. I accidentally discharged a firearm near spilled gasoline. Now the trailer's on fire. Oh, did I mention? Tim's handcuffed to the trailer. Looks like you're batting 0 for 3 in the family-saving department."

Eric froze. Fallows wanted to lure him out into the open. If he went, Fallows would kill him. If he didn't, Tim would die.

Fallows felt the burn of adrenalin pumping through his body. He inhaled deeply, enjoying the smell of burning gasoline, the feeling of lives teetering, the weight of the gun in his hand heavy and powerful as a broad axe.

Tim struggled against the handcuffs, his wrists raw and bleeding. The fire seemed to grow bigger with each inch it took closer to him. Tim's clothes were soaked with sweat from the heat, from fear.

"Don't worry, Tim," Fallows said. "I'll finish him off before the fire gets you. I hope." He winked and ducked around the side of the trailer, stalking Eric.

No one was there, though he could see fresh blood where Eric had fallen. Not much. A scraped elbow's worth. He moved cautiously, keeping his eye on what was now the roof of the trailer. At the far corner of the trailer, he spotted the toe of Eric's shoe barely visible.

He laughed. "Old trick, Eric." He shot the toe and the empty shoe flew to the side. "Is that your best? Hell, I taught you that one, remember?" Fallows kept walking, slowly moving around the trailer. "All you've proved so far is you can walk barefoot—"

The door to the trailer, which was now the roof, popped open and smoke and flame billowed up, and amongst the smoke and flame, Eric lunged out at Fallows like an escapee from hell. He rammed Fallows in the chest with his head, sending both of them sprawling to the ground. The Walther spun out of Fallows' hand and skidded across the pavement. The flames consumed most of the trailer now and lit their battleground brightly.

Blows were exchanged, fancy kicks, leg sweeps, reverse side kicks, plain old right hooks. Both men fought expertly, trying to use the hundred ways they knew of to kill a man on each other. Eric could only think of finishing it quickly in time to save Tim. But Fallows was too good to finish quickly. Eric might win the fight but lose Tim. He would have his revenge then, but Tim would be dead. But if Fallows won, he would save Tim. Maybe that was Tim's only hope, for Eric to lose this fight.

They were locked together, hands choking each other when a bullet zinged off the pavement near their feet.

They looked up.

Tim stood holding the Walther, aiming it at both of them. Soot covered his face and there was a nasty burn on his arm.

Eric and Fallows both took a step toward him.

Tim fired another round at the ground between them. "Don't. Either of you." He kept changing the position of the gun between Eric and Fallows. "I don't care which of you wins. I could have fried there for all either of you cared. From now on I'm on my own. I've learned enough from both of you that I could raise my own army, an army of kids like me. We could take whatever we want, whenever we want. And no one will stop us."

"I like the sound of that, Tim," Fallows said. "Let me help you. Like I said, there are a couple of things I still haven't taught you."

Tim smiled and Eric recoiled. His smile no longer resembled Annie's. It was a cold indifferent smile like a burrowing animal who's lucked into a nest of insects.

"Tim," Eric said.

"What?"

But he had nothing to add. There were no words that could convince a boy in Tim's condition. It surprised Eric, saddened him deeply, but he had nothing to say to his own son.

Tim turned and fled.

Eric and Fallows faced each other.

"This changes things," Fallows said. "I guess the winner goes after him."

Eric answered with a left hook that rocked Fallows. But Fallows recovered quickly and struck Eric with a hard blow. Again the two men struggled, their fighting taking them around the trailer to the burning jeep. Both men were tired, battered, staggering slightly as they clashed again and again. Their faces were splotched with dark knobs. Ribs were cracked, fingers broken, knuckles fractured.

Finally, Fallows faked a leg sweep which Eric dodged, and instead blasted out with a roundhouse kick that swiveled Eric's head around to the sound of crackling vertebrae. Eric fell to the ground and Fallows leaped on his back.

"I told your kid I had a few tricks left," he said, pulling out a strand of barbed wire and looping it around Eric's neck. He yanked hard and the sharp barbs punctured Eric's throat, spurting blood from each hole.

Eric felt the wire tightening. As his own strength weakened, Fallows seemed to get stronger. Eric gulped for air, but the wire cut any off. He tried to stand, but he had trouble distinguishing between his legs and his arms. He wasn't sure which did what. He searched his mind for a memory, a good one to die on. A time when he was with his family and they all smiled like people, not animals.

The image of Tim's feral smile ballooned in his mind. The greedy glint in his eyes as he described what he was going to do, his army of scavengers, crusaders without cause except their own gratification. And Tim would do it. He had the ability, the brains. He would someday run an army worse than Fallows'.

And that Eric couldn't endure.

He owed Annie better. He owed Tim better.

Eric felt the power starting somewhere deep within him, so deep it seemed to come from the center of the earth, traveling along some wire attached to Eric's navel. Wherever it came from, it grew and grew like a fireball until Eric was consumed in its energy.

He let out a growling roar and shook Fallows from his back.

Fallows still hung onto the wire, but Eric grabbed him by the belt with one hand and the throat with the other. The movement caused the barbs buried in his flesh to rake away lines of skin. Eric didn't notice. He hoisted Fallows into the air over his head and looked for someplace to hurl him.

The trailer was completely in flames now. There, on its underbelly, a few sharp rods of twisted metal stuck straight out like the horn of a giant unicorn. Eric ran toward that horn.

Holding Fallows high over his head, Eric thrust Fallows back-first onto the sharp end of the rods, impaling him there. Fallows' cried out in pain, but his grip on the wire around Eric's throat never loosened. Incredibly, the pain seemed to give him even greater strength.

Eric pushed harder. Fallows arched in agony, pulling even tighter. Eric felt his legs going numb but he pushed with all his might until the tip of the rods poked through Fallows' chest. Fallows looked down at the metal sticking out of his chest and smiled ruefully. He opened his mouth to say something, but nothing came out. He sagged into death, eyes open, hands still frozen to the barbed wire. Eric pried Fallows' hands from the wire, saw the deep holes where the barbs had burrowed into his palms.

Eric unwrapped the wire from his neck and breathed in deeply. He stared at Fallows' body suspended from the trailer, half-expecting him to climb down, laugh, and continue the fight. Even as the flames swept over Fallows' clothes and ignited him, melting him down to sizzling flesh, Eric stared, waiting.

Finally he accepted that Fallows was indeed dead.

He waited for some kind of feeling to enter his body. Relief. Joy. Justice. Vengeance.

Nothing came.

A great fiery explosion sounded behind him and Eric turned and saw the white shack with the missile and transmitting equipment go up in flames.

And even louder than the explosion came D.B.'s triumphant, *"Yahoooo!"*

Eric smiled.

25

"What's the problem?" Eric asked.

Wendy hobbled around the unconscious elephant and picked up the sledgehammer. She carried it back and placed it next to the chisel and crowbar. She picked up the quarter-inch electric drill and checked the connection to the battery. "No problem. Dizzy has a bad tooth that has to come out."

"So this is how you do it?" Eric moved closer, impressed with the deftness with which Wendy examined the elephant's mouth.

"You a hands-on observer, or just a commentator?"

Eric knelt next to the elephant. "What do you want me to do?"

"Hold his mouth open. This is a rush job. The tranquilizer won't last forever."

"Where's D.B.?"

"Practicing sign language with Madonna. She wants to teach her the lyrics to 'I Want to Hold Your Hand.' "

Wendy positioned the drill against the elephant's tooth. Suddenly she stopped, looked up at Eric. "You're going, aren't you?"

"And leave poor Dizzy with a cavity?"

"I mean soon. Today, tomorrow?"

Eric nodded.

She turned back to the tooth. Thin blue veins stood out in her temple. "Things too quiet for you around here?"

"Quiet? You call capturing Siberian tigers and a Komodo monitor quiet? I'd rather face graverobbers any day."

"It's only been two days."

"I can't risk any more time. Each day takes Tim further away. Most of the animals are caught again here. You're doing better. D.B.'s fine."

"Right, nothing to hold you here." She flicked on the drill and pressed it into the tooth for a few seconds.

Eric pulled her around. "He's my son."

"Why? Because you raised him? Maybe he's who he wants to be now. Maybe he isn't brainwashed or conditioned. Maybe he's just who he would have been anyway. You aren't the first middle-class parent whose kid has gone bad."

"Hey, guys, watch!" D.B. called excitedly. She ran up, pulling Madonna by the hand. "Watch this."

The ape sat down and picked at the fur on her arm.

"Fascinating," Eric said.

"Come on, Madonna. Show them." D.B. made some hand gestures. Finally, Madonna repeated them. "There! See? 'I' and 'hold.' I'm telling ya, kid, I'm gonna make you a star."

Eric and Wendy laughed.

"Tomorrow we work on 'hand,'" D.B. said. "I think I can get her to use all three in the right order in a week."

Neither Eric nor Wendy commented.

"What's up?" D.B. asked. "Oh. It's time to go, huh? And you're gonna tell me I'm better off staying. Right?"

"Right."

"And you think I'm gonna beg you to come along, don't you. That I'm crazy enough to leave this place where there's food and walls and water and go with you hunting your kid who punched me in the mouth and swiped my Playtex sling-shot."

Eric didn't say anything.

"Are you?" Wendy asked her. "Are you going to go with him? I've told you you're welcome to stay."

Loud banging on the wood barricade at the front of the zoo interrupted them.

Eric and D.B. grabbed their weapons and ran for the gates. Wendy limped quickly behind them using the crutches Eric had made for her.

Eric stood at the gate with his crossbow cocked. Several fists pounded on the door.

"What do you want?" Eric said.

"Let us in," the voice begged. "We have wounded."

D.B. shouldered her SMG.

Eric held up his hand for her to hold her fire. He opened the peephole he'd put in yesterday. A skinny old man carrying a spear stood in front of

232

the door. On the ground sat a young girl of six or seven. A woman in her late-thirties wore a harness and was dragging an Indian-style sled made from branches and a sheet. In the sled lay an unconscious boy in his late teens. He looked feverish.

"Can you help us?" the old man said. "My grandson's in bad shape."

Wendy hobbled up to the gate. She closed the peephole without looking through it. "I'm sorry. We have no help for you here."

"He's in bad shape," the old man repeated. He didn't seem to know what else to say.

Wendy looked at Eric. "I don't have supplies for everybody who comes this way. We take them in, we'll have to take everybody in. Soon they'll be slaughtering my animals."

"Your zoo, your decision," Eric said.

Wendy shook her head. "Why'd you come here?" she called.

"That kid sent us."

"What kid?" Eric asked.

"The one who shot my grandson. Sneaked into our camp last night and stole a bunch of food and clothes. Jimmy here took after him with a shotgun, but the kid shot Jimmy and took the shotgun too. Told Jimmy you folks might help."

Eric swung the gates open.

"Once," Wendy said. "Just this once."

Wendy and Eric took the boy to the infirmary and treated him immediately.

Afterward, the old man asked how the boy was doing.

"We'll know better in the morning."

The old man nodded and his daughter sat next

to the boy and watched him sleep.

Outside, Eric gathered his gear. Wendy and D.B. watched.

"He's my son. I brought him into this world. But if this is what he's going to do, I'll take him out."

"He's a boy," D.B. said.

"He almost killed another boy."

"But he sent them here. He could have left the kid to die. He didn't. He sent them here."

Eric nodded. Tim still had some of Eric and some of Fallows in him. He would have to find him before what was Eric and Annie were gone forever. Digging that bullet out of the young boy made Eric feel almost as if he'd shot the boy himself.

Eric hefted the pack on his back and slung the crossbow on his shoulders. D.B. turned and ran into the trailer where Madonna now lived. When she came out again, she had her backpack on.

"I've been packed since yesterday." She looked at Eric. "No arguments?"

"None."

Eric and Wendy didn't kiss. They didn't shake. He hugged her close and she hugged him back and for that time they seemed closer than if they'd been making love.

As she let them out the front gate, Wendy hooked a thumb over her shoulder toward the room where the family kept watch of the wounded boy. "Paradise will never be the same with people in it."

"Then it isn't paradise."

They left, Eric leading the way. D.B. waved

back at Wendy and Madonna for nearly ten minutes as they hiked away from the zoo.

Four hours later Eric and D.B. were eating a cooked rabbit and sipping catnip tea.

"I may go back there someday," D.B. said. "I mean to live."

"I may too," Eric said.

"Yeah? That paradise stuff is catching, huh?"

Eric cut a piece of rabbit off and handed it to her. "Right now this is all you need to know of paradise."

"And all I want to know," D.B. said, sinking her teeth into the meat.

THE BEST IN SUSPENSE FROM ZEBRA
by Jon Land

THE DOOMSDAY SPIRAL (1481, $3.50)

Tracing the deadly twists and turns of a plot born in Auschwitz, Alabaster — master assassin and sometime Mossad agent — races against time and operatives from every major service in order to control and kill a genetic nightmare let loose in America!

THE LUCIFER DIRECTIVE (1353, $3.50)

From a dramatic attack on Hollywood's Oscar Ceremony to the hijacking of three fighter bombers armed with nuclear weapons, terrorists are out-gunning agents and events are outracing governments. Minutes are ticking away to a searing blaze of earth-shattering destruction!

VORTEX (1469-4, $3.50)

The President of the US and the Soviet Premier are both helpless. Nuclear missiles are hurtling their way to a first strike and no one can stop the top-secret fiasco — except three men with old scores to settle. But if one of them dies, all humanity will perish in a vortex of annihilation!

MUNICH 10 (1300, $3.95)
by Lewis Orde

They've killed her lover, and they've kidnapped her son. Now the world-famous actress is swept into a maelstorm of international intrigue and bone-chilling suspense — and the only man who can help her pursue her enemies is a complete stranger . . .

DEADFALL (1400, $3.95)
By Lewis Orde and Bill Michaels

The two men Linda cares about most, her father and her lover, entangle her in a plot to hold Manhattan Island hostage for a billion dollars ransom. When the bridges and tunnels to Manhattan are blown, Linda is suddenly a terrorist — except *she's* the one who's terrified!

Available wherever paperbacks are sold, or order direct from the Publisher. Send cover price plus 50¢ per copy for mailing and handling to Zebra Books, Dept. 1697, 475 Park Avenue South, New York, N.Y. 10016. DO NOT SEND CASH.

ASHES
by William W. Johnstone

OUT OF THE ASHES   (1137, $3.50)
Ben Raines hadn't looked forward to the War, but he knew it was coming. After the balloons went up, Ben was one of the survivors, fighting his way across the country, searching for his family, and leading a band of new pioneers attempting to bring America OUT OF THE ASHES.

FIRE IN THE ASHES   (1310, $3.50)
It's 1999 and the world as we know it no longer exists. Ben Raines, leader of the Resistance, must regroup his rebels and prep them for bloody guerilla war. But are they ready to face an even fiercer foe—the human mutants threatening to overpower the world!

ANARCHY IN THE ASHES   (1387, $3.50)
Out of the smoldering nuclear wreckage of World War III, Ben Raines has emerged as the strong leader the Resistance needs. When Sam Hartline, the mercenary, joins forces with an invading army of Russians, Ben and his people raise a bloody banner of defiance to defend earth's last bastion of freedom.

BLOOD IN THE ASHES   (1537, $3.50)
As Raines and his ragged band of followers search for land that has escaped radiation, the insidious group known as The Ninth Order rises up to destroy them. In a savage battle to the death, it is the fate of America itself that hangs in the balance!

Available wherever paperbacks are sold, or order direct from the Publisher. Send cover price plus 50¢ per copy for mailing and handling to Zebra Books, Dept. 1697, 475 Park Avenue South, New York, N.Y. 10016. DO NOT SEND CASH.

THE SURVIVALIST SERIES
by Jerry Ahern

THE BEST IN ADVENTURES FROM ZEBRA

GUNSHIPS #2: FIRE FORCE (1159, $2.50)
by Jack Hamilton Teed

A few G.I.s, driven crazy by the war-torn hell of Vietnam, had banded into brutal killing squads who didn't care whom they shot at. Colonel John Hardin, tapped for the job of wiping out these squads, had to first forge his own command of misfits into a fighting FIRE FORCE!

GUNSHIPS #3: COBRA KILL (1462, $2.50)
by Jack Hamilton Teed

Having taken something from the wreckage of the downed Cobra gunship, the Cong force melted back into the jungle. Colonel John Hardin was going to find out what the Cong had taken — even if it killed him!

THE BLACK EAGLES #3:
NIGHTMARE IN LAOS (1341, $2.50)
by John Lansing

There's a hot rumor that Russians in Laos are secretly building a nuclear reactor. And the American command isn't overreacting when they order it knocked out — quietly — and fast!

THE BLACK EAGLES #4: PUNGI PATROL (1389, $2.50)
by John Lansing

A team of specially trained East German agents — disguised as U.S. soldiers — is slaughtering helpless Vietnamese villagers to discredit America. The Black Eagles, the elite jungle fighters, have been ordered to stop the butchers before our own allies turn against us!

THE BLACK EAGLES #5:
SAIGON SLAUGTHER (1476, $2.50)

Pulled off active operations after having been decimated by the NVA, the Eagles fight their own private war of survival in the streets of Saigon — battling the enemy assassins who've been sent to finish them off!

Available wherever paperbacks are sold, or order direct from the Publisher. Send cover price plus 50¢ per copy for mailing and handling to Zebra Books, Dept. 1697, 475 Park Avenue South, New York, N.Y. 10016. DO NOT SEND CASH.